The Bhabhis Of Lahore

&

other forbidden tales of the city

Ayesha Muzaffar

LIBERTY Publishing

Published by Liberty Publishing

C-16, Sector 31-A Mehran Town Extension,

Korangi Industrial Area, Karachi – Pakistan

First published in Pakistan 2022

Copyright © Ayesha Muzaffar 2022

1 2 3 4 5 6 7 8 9 10

ISBN 978-969-8729-783

This book is dedicated to

Ama jee [Sanila Muzaffar] - the wonderfully persuasive woman who wanted me to pursue a double masters in finance, but ended up with her daughter writing a book about the hidden horrors instead.

Baba jee [Malik Muzaffar] - the man who now spends his days crafting beautiful bits of urdu poetry and making afghani dishes in the kitchen (each with as many tomatoes as possible).

Nani ama - the woman who refuses to age, and also expresses her love by showering me with exquisite bed sheet sets that make me never want to wake up.

Farhan - my darling husband who thinks that having a wife who chuckles to herself at night is not comical.

Zeba ami - a saas who knits wonders for me at Zohra.B.

Aamir abu - with whom I share the love of chocolate milk powders.

Momo - the sister behind Sugar Scoop, Lahore's finest gelato.

Hajra - the (not so) little bundle of joy who is always the first to gobble up my tales.

Tales

Prologue

We live in a magnificent country, one which is full of curious beings and sheltered stories that roam in the whispers amongst those beings. I bring to you such stories that make ama's and aba's eyes pop open - as if they have seen a ghost, which they have not - but these tales, in all their glamour, are not those to be retold. Yet I have taken upon myself such a task. Tales of heartbreak, of men who deserved better, of women who loved too dearly, of centuries old dusty mattresses covered with newly purchased silk sheets that bounce to this day, of jinns and their families, and of course - living, breathing tales of you and me and all of us.

However, before I begin, I would like to mention a few, very random people that have absolutely nothing to do with the creation of this book, but have played a valuable role in my life at one point or another and so I shall talk about them.

In Canal View society, a society not very hidden in Lahore, old to its core, there is a Poly Clinic around the corner of a street. The doctor who runs it used to greet his patients with the grandest smile, but now his hanging skin and delicately frail bones (still covered with a good amount of fat) do not allow him to laugh and welcome us as openly as he once did. His name is Dr. Nasir, and he is a man of magic. He makes his patients drink a mixture of potions and injects liquids into those who have been battling for the longest time, or those who have been so ill that they have forgotten what being well feels like, and within a span of days, you and I, and all those that he treats, return back to normal, *better than normal,* as if nothing had ever happened. I was the child who invited diseases with names I cannot pronounce, and it was him, Dr. Great Nasir, who from his tiny, almost unkempt clinic, drove me back to life.

There is a friend of mine, whose father used to own a school van and on days when my parents were occupied, I used to sit in that white van, with a Convent of Jesus and Mary sticker plastered on the back and reach home. The school I was not fond of, still am not, for it gave some terrible memories, but that ride home was nothing short of a splendid time; the sticky ice-lolly liquid dripping down my chin, talks of teachers and their pets, and the usual jump in the air each time the driver sped past a speedbreaker. That friend, her name is Amna, and she is a bundle of joy, and though we have not met in the longest time, she is full of sincere opinions and happy thoughts.

The third mention is of a woman whose name I do not know because to me, she was always KFC *wali aunty,* and her house was somewhere unknown, where lots of tangled electrical wires hung outside and children ran with the vehicles passing by. She is still alive, but not in Pakistan. However, when she was here, she was my nano's closest *saheli,* and back when we were ten, when fast food meals only happened on Eids, she used to pamper us with buckets of KFC *botis* and Zinger burgers. Again, this is the time when our biggest pleasure was ten rupee pops after school hours. Each time we went, which at one time was twice each week for almost a year, we were welcomed by the aroma of spicy Kentucky chicken and though now I have Mandarin's sticky garlic rice and Chop Chop Wok's sushi as comfort food, those times were the best. Thank you, KFC wali aunty.

Before I got married, we used to have a driver uncle called Kamran. He had a sinister wife who beat her two year old child - the darling creature who would wait by the gate for his father to return at night. Though quite petite, with the voice of a hushed woman, Kamran uncle made several years of my family's lives utterly peaceful. From delivering the bakery's buttercream cakes when my sister had not yet mastered the art of an intact buttercream covering, dropping me to business school a good forty minutes away and always being on time to pick me up, to making the best Biryani on Sundays with half-peeled potatoes and homemade masalas, Kamran uncle is a man that I cannot forget. But I am happy that he is gone, for now as I have heard, he is somewhere in the mountains where he always longed to be, driving tourists to spots and offering them some good ol' biryani.

The Bhabhis of Lahore

Our family is full of odd happenings, doings, and the strangest of beings. For instance, when I was young, I was told that we belonged to a cast that had been erased from the city and that we could only meet our people far off in the mountains. And so, every Eid when my friends went to the northern areas and stayed in posh hotels and resorts, we went to unknown peaks and lived amongst yellow-throated marten. If I think hard enough and close my eyes, I can feel the mountain sunlight chasing my skin, and if I keep thinking, I can taste the pale-colored, yogurt-like treat that nana jaan used to feed me. There were times when he'd forget the spoon and make balls of the sweet treat using his fingers – his fingers were salty. I yearn for it: the sweet and then the salt. I have gone to grocery stores across the globe; Chinese marts, Indian vendors, exotic milk sellers from Iceland but none can match the flavor. I have had people place their creations in my mouth and I have licked their fingers, but nothing has hit home. Magic milk I call it. I have no one to ask about it. Ama disappeared after the death of baba jaan and chacha moved to Karachi. Bhai, the only person I live with, recalls nothing.

Bhai and I are nestled in the heart of Lahore and our old house, except my ama's room which still smells like her after a decade, has been renovated. Bhai let it be because he feels that ama still visits from time to time. 'We may not see her, but her presence can be felt – in the creaking of the wooden stairs, the breeze that escapes inside when I shut the windows, and in *you*. You look exactly like her.' I do not want to resemble the woman who fed me lies and twisted my nipples but bhai says that ama loved me and on cold nights when I have nothing happy to think about, I believe him. Bhai is a wondrous person and a rather fascinating archeologist. In the morning, when I sit by the curtains and write stories, bhai goes on adventures and brings back peculiar stones and ornaments. He then cleans them with much precision and hands them to the museum the next day. 'You act like these belongings are so valuable to you and yet you are so quick to hand them over' I often say. 'It is never good to keep something that you do not know the history of. Things have souls too,' he replies. I nod in approval but of course, we do not think alike. I wanted to grow up and look like him, be like him, but knowing how his life has unraveled, I do not wish for it anymore. For the strangers who are reading this tale, telling you that bhai spends many Sundays at the orphanage, never raises his voice, and feeds stray cats gourmet meals that he cooks for fun, speaks a lot about who he is. But, he also has six broken marriages; six women who were not happy with him and six bhabhis who I often bump into as I stroll across the Lahori streets.

Before baba jaan died, he married off bhai at the age of eighteen to our cousin Bushra. She was great at

UNO and adored watching drama serials with ama jaan. My parents loved her as much as bhai did, if not more. I would often see bhai and Bushra bhabhi playing badminton in the park where my sole duty was to fetch the shuttlecock if the wind carried it away. Sometimes bhai would purposely throw it in the bushes so that he could run to bhabhi and grab her from behind. Bhabhi would giggle and break free when she'd see me returning. Just eight months later, bhabhi jee ran away with a boy. He was someone she had met at the park and they ran away when bhai was attending a math lecture at his college. Bhai was heartbroken but ama said that he was too young to realize what love was and that his heart was perfectly intact. The family ties with phupho were cut, and ama seemed to be at peace about it. 'She was not the right one,' she told bhai. 'She thought of men like winter sweaters. If not blue then pink. But we all know how terrible the color pink is. It wears out and so will her man.' Phupho found her daughter and dragged her back. Bhai wanted to forgive her and Bushra bhabhi wanted to be forgiven, but ama did not let it happen. Years later, I saw Bushra bhabhi at Liberty market. She was pregnant, radiant, and licking a Paradise cone.

The second wedding was a grand one, perhaps the grandest and most spectacular wedding I have attended to this date. It was also the one that lasted the *longest* – two years. It took place six months after the first one and was with a jeweler's daughter. He was baba's close friend – the type we had heard fond memories about. Sehar's father, who I to this day deeply respect, showered us with immense kindness and well, gold. He purchased a house in the newly made phase 4 in DHA Lahore for the newly-weds. Bhai has always been a man who knows how to love, but with Sehar bhabhi it was as he terms it, as hard as learning to love a rock, whatever that meant. 'Even rocks are lovable,' bhai said. 'But this woman cannot be loved.' Sehar bhabhi, a woman who had majored in mental sciences and ran a part-time clinic of her own, could not trust bhai. She spied on him, wept when she had *dreams* of bhai cheating on her, and drove the maids away thinking that they would all fall in love with her husband. It got to the extent that Sehar bhabhi's father, uncle jee started sending groceries and paying bills because bhabhi number two would not and could not let bhai leave the house without her. 'My Sehar was never like this,' uncle jee told us. 'And my son is not the man she thinks he is,' my then critically ill baba replied. 'It is all in her head.' One humid night, in the midst of Ramadan when my mouth was stuffed with an omelet, we had to rush to the hospital. We knew that bhai had tripped and fallen down the stairs but when he gained consciousness, we learned that it was Sehar bhabhi who had pushed him. 'I was going to lock the doors and then I heard Sehar accusing me of wanting to leave her for another woman and then…' Bhai did not say anything more. The stitches on the wound dissolved but there's still a patch of brown on bhai's forehead from that day. Every time he notices it, he shrugs. The last time I saw bhabhi was in court, and she did not look that well.

'The next time I bring a woman into this house, it will be on my terms,' bhai said. 'Of course, it will be on *your* terms,' ama jaan snapped. 'Your baba is now dead. The last two choices were his. Pink and rotten.' For the next two years, bhai focused on his career – he was fixated on making something of himself, *till* he saw her. Majhbeen. 'God molded her to perfection. She is like a fair maiden. Her skin is the color of milk, her eyes the shape of almonds and she blinks too often – it is like seeing a butterfly flap its wings, it is like she cuts short what she wants to see, *blink, blink,* snippets, and holds onto them. Little snippets of me.' I knew that bhai had blindly fallen in love because Majhbeen bhabhi looked nothing like a maiden – she was a woman twice bhai's age and she could barely keep her eyes open. I wanted to sit her down, make her look up, and take out whatever was stuck in her eyes. Before bhai could make her meet ama, ama jee disappeared. Ama jee had started acting out weeks before, and we thought that it was because of baba's death, but when husbands die, wives do not act like ama did. For instance, she would ask bhai if he could pretend that he was baba and sleep next to her. 'I can sleep next to you as your son too,' bhai said. 'If you need company that is.' But ama was adamant about pretending that bhai was baba. This turned the once homely atmosphere into a rather uncomfortable one. Ama hardly talked to me unless it was regarding bhai and even then she would fantasize about him being baba. 'Go Sarfraz, get baba jaan some water,' she would say and point towards bhai.

One morning we woke up to not find her in the house. We looked for weeks. The entire neighborhood searched for her. During this time, Majhbeen *aunty*, who was bhai's friend, became his lover. Ama's disappearance brought them closer. Aunty jee had only one sister she considered family so the marriage ceremony was done in our society's mosque with a few of bhai's friends and aunty jee's sister. The morning after bhai's marriage, which was rather similar to the morning of ama's disappearance, with foggy, unclear skies, no electricity, and an awful stomach ache, Majhbeen aunty woke up screaming. At first, she asked bhai why all the lights were turned off and when bhai pulled back the curtains and turned on all lights, Majhbeen aunty could still not see a thing. It was also the first time she wasn't blinking like a mad woman – bhai's butterflies were asleep. For some moments aunty jee was quiet, but then she started screaming when she realized that she had lost her eyesight. Horrible, horrible screams. Bhai was upset of course, for he loved her and so he took it upon himself to take care of her when we were told that she would never be able to see. We had caretakers, but bhai did most of her work as any loving husband would. Eventually, the doctors had her shifted to Sialkot and bhai landed his first proper job after losing his football factory startup because of Sehar bhabhi. Things became slow and irksome but bhai still made the effort to be there for her and *then,* after nine months of togetherness and blindness, she made a *request.* She asked bhai to divorce her and marry her sister instead because she was all Majhbeen aunty worried about. Bhai was reluctant at first, but he was tired and after some time (a rather short time), he accepted. Of course, he would not stop caring for Majhbeen aunty – if not as her husband, then as her brother-in-law.

When the fourth woman came into bhai's life, I became an introvert. The three former bhabhis, ama's phantom act, and the search for a non-existent milk treat made me want to shun everyone out and so I did. Mano bhabhi, who was the first to realize that I no longer was what I used to be when her sister was around, started to act worried. Of course, she did not know me and so it was all a show; English breakfasts for me – round pancakes and fancy eggs, movie tickets to Khan films, and staying up at night to help me with intermediate exams, she did it all. Bhai liked it. I did not but because of him, I *let* it happen. I *let* it happen. I let Mano bhabhi come close to me, so much so that she fell in love with me and the three strands of hair I called a beard. Bhai heard it from his own ears and saw it from his own eyes – an overly excited Mano bhabhi talking on the phone with a saheli and going on and on about how she would love to make love to me and how she imagined it when she was doing *it* with bhai. Bhai divorced her the month after. I see her a lot. Perhaps it is because she lives nearby or that the entire Lahore gathers at Mall 1 for entertainment and there she usually is; exposing her yellow teeth in a grin that is as revolting as it gets.

Bhai made it clear that he was not fit for marriage. 'You are the best man I know,' I told him. 'And you make the very best husband.' It was true that things had not worked out in his favor, but bhai had never been at fault. Well – at least until his fifth marriage. We were both determined that none of us were good judges, which is why we came to the conclusion that an important decision such as choosing a life partner should be left to someone else. Someone wise, someone with an expertise in the area – and someone we could *blame* if things didn't work out. We met with a *rishta* aunty, a matchmaker as many call her, and had her arrange potential matches for bhai. 'He is good looking, he has money and there is no mother in the picture. Things look great. However...'

'However?'

'However, he has been married four times and no one will give their daughter to such a man,' she said.

'That is your job,' I said. 'To make them see that bhai was never wrong and that she will be the happiest woman alive.'

'Hmm. I will have to charge a lot extra for this.'

'That is not a problem.'

It took four months for the first match to arrive. She was a divorced doctor with two children. She appeared to be pretty decent and bhai had no problem with the children but when bhai met her, he realized that she had no interest in marriage and that she was being forced into it. The second match came a week after and it was of an eighteen-year-old from a financially poor background. Bhai refused at once. The matchmaker insisted that I should meet her but shook my head. 'I am not looking for love.' Which was true, I was not. I had stopped believing in it. After that, several proposals came but bhai did not feel comfortable proceeding with any. For instance, there was one he was inclined towards but the woman mentioned that she was an atheist and that bhai had to promise her that all their children would be non-believers. After some time, the matchmaker brought home photos of a young woman and the moment I saw bhai looking at the photos, I *knew* that chum-chums were bouncing in his stomach. Her name was Riffah and she was a teacher at a convent school. When she sat across from the table at dinner for the first time, we thought we had known each other for ages. As if, she had always been there. At the end of the year, Riffah bhabhi and bhai were married. It should be noted that though the marriage did not work out, Riffah bhabhi was one of the most genuine women I had ever had the pleasure of knowing and if I ever do get married, I will want to find someone like her.

Riffah bhabhi loved bhai. She thought of him as the sun and the moon and everything in between and slowly, bhai grew very fond of her. I had never seen bhai *this* content. She was a simple woman and she knew how to run a house and make her man happy. There was nothing more to it. After some time, Riffah bhabhi requested bhai to take her to the doctor. 'Are you ill?' bhai asked. 'Is everything alright, meri jaan?' Bhabhi nodded her head. 'You know how terribly I want a child. I am already thirty. I need to go to the doctor.' And so, bhai took her to Lahore's top clinic the very next day. The doctor ran some tests and ruled out all complications. 'Your health is perfect. Just pray to God and you'll be blessed anytime now. And oh, get the mister checked as well.' Bhai took an off and went for his tests. Bhabhi spent the day fixing the wardrobes and deciding which room the nursery would be. When she chose the color peach, we also got bhai's results. There were a lot of red, out-of-range figures on the paper. 'It is alright,' Riffah bhabhi replied, seeing the results. 'We will get them done again from another lab.' It was fine for us, but Riffah bhabhi did not sleep that night. Eventually, after a series of doctor visits, it was concluded that bhai *could never* be a father. No treatment guaranteed results. Within the next two months, Riffah bhabhi hugged bhai farewell and begged him for a divorce. 'I *need* children,' she said. 'I cannot wait.' 'I love you,' bhai replied. 'I am sure we can work it out.' They could not work it out. Riffah bhabhi now has a child – a son or daughter, I do not know but I have heard that she despises her husband. The neighbors often hear them threatening to kill each other. But yes, she has a child.

At this point, both bhai and I refrained from mentioning marriage or anything leading to marriage in the house. It was strictly work, and well, sometimes a game of badminton outside. 'I think I am cursed,' bhai once said as he swung the racket behind him. 'All this is not normal.' 'There is nothing abnormal about it,' I replied. 'But it is fine. It is not the end of the world.' A lot of men would have ended up sharing the same fate as bhai had they not given up after the first or second failed relationship. 'It is good that you allow your heart to heal and then go at it again. This is how you will find true love,' I said. Bhai scoffed. We both knew I believed little in what I was saying.

Bhai and I had given up on the quest to find bhai a woman, but the universe had other plans. I recall that it was early February and the news of a weird flu-like virus had taken the world by storm. Most of bhai's international trips were canceled and he was assigned to lead the new office in Gujrat. 'Bhai,' I said when I phoned him after a week. 'I have heard that this virus, Corona as they call it, has arrived in Pakistan. I think you should come back home.' 'I think I will stay for a bit,' came a reply. His tone was hesitant and I instantly knew that either a) there was someone in the room with him who was making him talk like this, or b) he was hiding something. It turned out that both the options were correct. Bhai was in the room with a woman, Feroza, and he was hiding the fact that she had shown interest in him and proposed that they get married.

'You have known her for seven days. *Seven days!* And out of the blue, she has asked for you to marry her. It is rather odd,' I said. 'For all we know she could be a man,' I snapped.

'I assure you that she is not a man.'

'But *who* is she?'

'I-I don't know much. All I know is that for seven days we have worked together and that she has liked me and I have liked her. She is the first woman who *actually* wants me to marry her.'

'She wants you to jump to such a big commitment without knowing her?'

'I knew all the others,' bhai replied. 'Look where that got me. I have told her about it.'

'About your other wives?'

'That too… But about my sperm count.'

'Oh, alright.'

'Listen…' I continued. 'I am happy if you're happy.'

'I am happy.'

Feroza had been married before but of course just once, not as many times as bhai had. She was a chirpy woman, who spoke too soon and too much. She belonged to a family of some famous bakers in Multan, and she believed that unicorns were real. She was a child at heart and perhaps that is what bhai had wanted all along. 'I knew that he was the one when I saw him!' she exclaimed with joy. 'When you know, you just know!' *If only we ever did know.*

Feroza's family was overjoyed because they had not thought that they would ever find someone to like Feroza. 'She's a ball of energy,' her sister said. 'And there is only so much energy you can stand.' I was suspicious about why the parents had agreed so fast but then I got to spend time with Feroza *bhabhi* and I had a terrible headache – the kind no Panadol can cure. She was too much. The thought of living in the same house as her annoyed me – she was a woman with children aged from three to fifteen, all inside of her, swinging between a hyper childhood and troubling puberty. But in the end, bhai was happy so that was all that mattered. Even if it meant becoming a blood pressure patient in my thirties.

The nikkah was done and all the travel documents procured a month before all the functions because bhai had some conferences to attend right after the events and he had made the most glorious decision of tagging his wife along with him. Sandwiched between the nikkah and the main events was a dua function that the bride's family had kept. A mufti sahab had to come and give his blessings and then there were some other family traditions that the elders wanted to do. I remember the day clearly. The hall was small and there were a lot of people. Clusters of aunties were gathered in each corner whispering among themselves and a rather frantic team of waiters with sweaty foreheads was running around handing out pineapple juice. Bhai and bhabhi were seated under the only AC, and when the mufti sahab arrived, he was given that place. In between the recitation, mufti sahab got up and started roaming across the hall. We assumed that he was feeling hot but shortly after he stopped talking and asked the bride's family to accompany him behind the stage. Every few seconds someone from Feroza bhabhi's family would go behind the gigantic flower vase and join the others. I sipped my pineapple juice. 'Now this is unusual,' I said under my breath. The food was served and the guests were then asked to leave. Bhai and I were still clueless. After most of the families left, mufti sahab called for us. 'This wedding does not have my blessing,' he said. 'This gentleman right here,' he said pointing to bhai. 'Is already married and the wife has not given permission for another marriage. Now, Islam permits four marriages but, in this case, marriage to daughter Feroza can be life-threatening for her.' I kept sipping my juice. I could have spoken, but I chose not to. I let bhai handle it. Bhai told them about all the marriages and how he was not in contact with any of them and he also brought forward a now weeping Feroza who said that whatever had been said was true.

'When I was reciting, I felt darkness in the room. I followed it. It was *his* wife. He has been married off as a child to a goat-jinn in the mountains. He has not returned to her and thus she is not letting any of his marriages work,' the mufti spoke.

'What nonsense!' Bhai cut in. 'Married to a what?'

'A goat jinn.'

Feroza bhabhi started weeping again.

'Come on, Feroza! You don't believe him, do you?'

Feroza bhabhi started crying harder.

'Get away from my daughter. Mufti sahab does not lie!' Bhabhi's khala yelled and pushed bhai to the side. 'With you around, she may never lead a promising life!'

'Easy there aunty,' I said. 'Let us sit and talk.'

Bhai pulled mufti sahab to the side. 'What is it that you want? Money? I will give you as much as you want!'

'Listen beta. I am telling you the truth. You need to know the problem to solve it. Return to the mountains and solve it.'

Feroza bhabhi and bhai stayed in contact for several weeks before she left for the US to pursue a degree. After that, she asked for a divorce. All the gifts we had sent were sent back to us with a Quran and some tasbeehs. It has been two years to this and bhai has not brought up the topic of marriage. We have also not visited the mountains. However, we did visit a religious scholar who said that phupho jaan, Bushra bhabhi's ama had done an *amal* that had led to ama losing her sanity and bhai's marriages ending in nuisance. Black magic, the magic milk, a goat-jinn or just fate, we do not know and we are not willing to find out. Unless… unless bhai falls in love again.

Mera Mehtab

Chapter
1

There are stories you see on screens, and then the ones that your khala tells you with spices and lies and whatnot, and then there are true as life stories that break your heart, and it upsets you to think of them without a happy ending, or exaggeration, and you try to forget such tales of utter disappointment. Because deep down, you live for the fairy tales and the masala – stories that give you a sense of longing. But, you see, life doesn't knit sweaters that fit – there's always an arm too long or a string hanging.

This story is of Momina Batool and her love for *mong phalli* and Mehtab. You see, when Momina was young, and could hardly hold a pen – when all her cousins called Mehtab, Mehtab *bhai,* Momina was instructed not to. 'He is everyone's *bhai* but yours,' her mother, Shamila begum instructed, as she swirled her daughter's silky hair into a braid. 'You will know when you grow up, but I do not want you calling him bhai. Call him Mehtab.'

'Mehtab,' little Momina repeated under her breath. She liked the sound of it.

'Yes,' Shamila begum answered. 'Say his name like you own it.'

Mehtab was six years older than little Momina, and he was a sharp child for his age. His mother was often seen handing hundred rupee notes to the workers, as a form of *sadqa* for her dear son. Mehtab's father had left them for another woman, and it was his mamoo, Momina's father, who looked after them all. Between whispers and chuckles, it had been decided in that old house of theirs, that Mehtab and Momina would be married when the time arrived. Mehtab's mother, Fouzia begum, also had an elder son, Zubair, but he wasn't half as bright as her youngest. Zubair studied, ate and slept, but he hardly talked. The doctors said that there was nothing wrong with him, and the massi said that he had no jinn, so it was declared that he was a rather boring soul, and there was no cure for that.

Mehtab and Zubair, though poles apart with one being soft like butter and other hard like the ghee in winter, adored each other and got along very well. Zubair had more of his father's face, and the habits of a boy who silently agreed but had no say, or thought. Mehtab was like the wind, as Fouzia begum termed it, hopping from one place to the next, and sometimes like the sun, for it was he who was the *ronak* of the house. As predicted, Zubair grew up to be a man of little words. He did his FSC in Science and went on to pursue medicine in Karachi. Fouzia begum although reluctant to send her son, abided by his wishes, for she knew deep down that having him in the house and not having him, were one and the same thing. But as Zubair went, Fouzia begum told her youngest, Mehtab, 'Zubair is mature and he knows the ways of the world. You do not so do not ever expect me to send you away from home like that.' It was clear that she could not part ways with a part of her heart.

Momina was not as wise or capable as her cousins. She already knew that she had a mind the size of a pea because she *almost* always passed, and when she focused too hard on what was written in the textbook, the numbers flew away from her reach – even when she wore spectacles. But, despite not knowing plural from singular, or how derivation was done – the very unimportant things in life, Momina grew up to be just fine. She went for arts, and when she was told that she could not draw faces, she drew Mehtab's room, and his watch, and his shaving kit, and all that he owned that she had seen. She was what God had made on a Sunday – just good looking with the most outlined lips, and pumped inside her was the energy of the world. With her around, everything and everyone worked out well.

Mehtab, a rather non-serious boy, with a knack for fixing things, from aunties AC's to Momina's mood, was more interested in social work, and running for the society's president – and later on the country's- grew up to look like flashing light. The kind that when looked at, needs to be looked at again. His most prominent features were his jaw and his oiled back hair that when not brushed, covered most of his hazel-colored eyes. He was and always had been against haircuts. Till Zubair was with him, Mehtab was forced to trim his hair as per society's acceptance, but now that his brother was out of the city, becoming a surgeon, Mehtab let his neck-length hair loose. Future presidents and makers of the law wore their hair as they pleased.

The entire family and let me inform you – it was a rather large one- knew of Mehtab and Momina. They knew what the elders had decided and they very well knew to not let their daughters fall for Mehtab – a boy they thought deserved someone better looking than plain old Momo. But the ones who knew her knew that she indeed was the only sweater that could fit Mehtab – and when needed would change shape and color, and shower him with the love he had missed out on. It was a match made by the after-rain-skies.

It so happened, that Zubair completed his studies and returned back to Lahore, Mehtab scraped past his graduation, only to be able to apply for CSS, and Momina went on a fancy *anda* diet she learned about on the internet, to fit into her bridal clothes. The children grew up in front of Fouzia and Shamila begum, and the time had come to wed them. Of course, Mehtab and Momina could not wait, for they were madly in love, and had been since birth, but it was decided that Zubair would be wedded first – he was the eldest after all. Fouzia begum had wanted him to like a girl, and she expected that he did, for she knew that finding him one would be a daunting task. It was not that he was not handsome, or well-educated – in fact, he was all that and more, but he was, as his mother termed it: empty.

The news spread and many women were interested – but their daughters, not so much. They all thought that he was occupied or in love with another woman, or god forbid, even queer – as he showed no interest. He tried to, truth be told – but Zubair was Zubair, and he could only put on an act for some time. A friend of Shamila begum's, who lived in the village, had befriended a woman, whose daughter was simple and well-mannered and knew less of the city – and she was deemed an ideal match for Zubair.

Zubair, of course, agreed to what his mother pleased.

He had only one wish: that he disliked noise and dances, and even though he had to dress up, having limited guests and a quieter venue would be appreciated. The begums frowned, for it was his wedding they wanted to rejoice on, but they let the thought pass, knowing that another couple, their favorite one, was to be wedded soon. And so, Zubair's wedding was an hour-long event in the food hall in Oasis, as far away from people, decorated by Mehtab and Momina, as per his liking – dim lights and the tune of Titanic, and absolutely no cake. The dishes at the end, although of many kinds, were to be distributed amongst the needy.

Laiba was beautiful. She was tall and fair, with eyes the size of buttons, and when she laughed, the laughter spiraled round and round like *jalebis* floating in sizzling hot oil. She loved to laugh on the tiniest of things and she laughed a lot. Even when she turned on the switch, and it blinked and fused, she managed to chuckle. She was a pure soul, and whenever anyone looked at her, she looked away, for she would always be looking at Zubair.

Laiba settled in well, and she adored the entire family. She welcomed Momina into her house, knowing that she was her sister-to-be. They sat together for hours on end, talking about things that needed no talking about – for that is what sisters did. In the second month of Laiba and Zubair's marriage, Momina made a portrait of them from her finest pastel colors, and even in the picture, she could not make Zubair smile.

'I don't know what his smile looks like,' Momina told his wife. 'Had I drawn it, it wouldn't have looked like Zubair bhai.'

Laiba smiled. 'It's alright, he's the happiest, and he just does not know how to show it.'

But that indeed was the problem. There was only so much Laiba could imagine and do. Zubair wasn't a bad partner – even though he did not speak, except when they wanted to make love, or turn on the lamp, or if he wanted a warm glass of milk which he wanted every day, so when Laiba started putting it on his bedside, he stopped uttering those words too – Zubair did like having Laiba around. In fact, between him and God, he was growing fonder of her day by day and he wanted to place the entire world at her feet. But of course – he did not say so.

Six months later, the wedding functions of Mehtab and Momina started. Most of the relatives were over and staying at both the houses, which I would like to add, were inter-joined. There was the *sangeet*, and the *sangeet* with the actual singer, and the *dholki*, that led to the *sangeet*, and the *duae-khair* after it, and these were all the unplanned events. If I had to describe that time and the place – it was the happiest, and perhaps if an angel had to descend from the heavens, he too would have chosen to stay in the house where Mehtab and Momnina were becoming one.

But my nano always said that in a box of the most perfect milk laddoos, there always is a laddoo crushed at the bottom- out of shape and if you go person to person, offering the box of sweets, no one would pick that laddoo, and at this moment in time, the laddoo was Laiba. Do not get me wrong – she was happy for Mehtab and even happier for Momina, but seeing what true love was saddened her. Without knowing, she felt like the laddoo nano talked about, for it had been months and she had not experienced it nor even sensed it, and she longed for it: Love.

On the night before Momina's big day, Laiba sat next to her, oiling her hair.

'Momina,' she said. 'When you call out Mehtab *bhai*, you make a funny face - why is that?'

'Oh,' Momina smiled, 'It isn't shame. It's knowing that I own it – the name and the person both. My ama taught me that. So I call it out with love and respect and ownership.'

Laiba ran her fingers through her friend's hair and let out a sigh.

'You should try it too,' Momina continued. 'Say Zubair bhai's name like you own it.'

'But I don't,' came a whisper, soft enough to be uttered but not loud enough for Momina to hear.

The next day, before the festivities commenced, Laiba kissed begum Fouzia's hand, who had woken up with a terrible dream, and said that she was going to fetch her mother from the station with the driver, and as Fouzia begum smiled at her and gave her approval – it was the last she ever saw of Laiba. Laiba never returned from her village – not for Momina's wedding, and not for any day after it.

'Living with him is like living with a wall,' she had scribbled on a *hisaab kitaab* register.

'And the village has many walls. I am better there.'

Chapter
2

'If you miss three *jumma* prayers, you become a *kaafir*,' Mehtab said, as he placed the prayer mat on the carpet.

'Astagfar,' Momina replied. "Rather than hurriedly offering the third in a row, why don't you stop missing the first two?"

He smirked. 'Duniya and deen saath saath, na.'

Momina nestled herself right next to her lover, and both of them prayed for Laiba *bhabhi's* return. The *nikkah* was to occur in the evening, and Fouzia begum, accompanied by a few relatives, had left for the village to fetch back Laiba. Zubair, who was away performing an operation on a toddler with six fingers – whose parents thought that he might be possessed - was oblivious to what was happening behind his back. As he scalped his way into giving the boy a normal hand, he spread his fingers and imagined the space between them being filled by Laiba's bread-like hand – the touch and scent of which he loved.

Even as a child, when given Eidi, Zubair had never known how to react. But, seeing that his mother was never seen happy around his now-gone father, he folded the notes and put them under his mother's pillow. He was the child who was seen as disrespectful for not being happy on Eidi, but folded under the old sheets had been fungus-covered notes, for it took him longer than others to understand what love is, but he did.

Fouzia begum returned in the evening, and without a word, got dressed in white and pearls, a color she wore when she was the happiest or the gloomiest – and today was a day for both. She did not know what to tell her son; that his wife had refused to come, or that she had not been able to find his wife – the latter was true. She was assured by her companions that Laiba would indeed return, for they had sensed her love for Zubair, but Fouzia begum thought otherwise for she knew how difficult it was to love her son.

It was said to all that Laiba had gone to be with her grandmother, bee begum, who was ill and on her death-bed and that no one should talk more about it. In good time, she would return. The attention was reverted back to the preparations: the stage was bright yellow with lilies of the best kind, sprayed so that the insects would not come, as it was the weather of bugs, restless nights, and uncertainties. Momina wore her mother's lehenga, the edges of which had been trimmed to match her height, paired with silver bangles, and a polished heirloom choker, and between the sky and the earth and all the beings between them, Momina looked ravishing. She made the most stunning bride and just watching her glide from one guest to another, effortlessly, made Fouzia begum's worries fade away.

That day, all the guests stood on chopped grass, wishing Mehtab and Momina a blessed life. The children who accompanied their parents sensed a belief in love, and it was truly as if God had written the ceremony in gold, and offered it on a platter.

Zubair, who returned at the time of the nikkah, and had made shaadi planners from Gujrat arrange the occasion according to his brother's wishes, came holding a bangle of gold with his initials next to his dear Laiba's, as a token of love. He had not thought of how he'd present it, or what he'd say – or that he might just leave it on the dressing table, but he had made sure it was the most expensive piece the finest jeweler in Anarkali had.

'Laiba's dado is very ill, she's dying,' said Fouzia begum. 'She left just some time ago, son.'

'With whom?' asked Zubair. 'Mama jaan, had you informed me, I would have come earlier and taken her.'

'I – she *did* not want to upset you. But it is alright, she said that she will come back after some time.'

'I should be with her,' said Zubair.

Astonished by his son's reaction, Fouzia begum interrupted him sternly. 'Nonsense, beta. You should be with your dear brother. Laiba strictly forbade us to let you follow. She said that she will let us know in a week.'

'A week!' gasped Zubair. 'I-'

It was what Fouzia begum had least expected: her son, empty as he had ever been, had fallen for his wife unknowingly. Seeing the various expressions on his rather plain face, upset her deeply. She bent forward and held his hand. 'Do not worry dear son, we will go and get her in a day or two.'

Zubair thrust the gold bracelet wrapped in silk deep into his coat pocket, and left without saying another word to his mother.

The entire society was lit up in the shiniest lights and had you been there, you would have known how marvelous and futuristic that marriage was – almost as if it had been held in today's time. The function ended late at night when the begamats could dance no more, and still, no one wanted to leave.

At night, Mehtab and Momina lay under the stars, holding hands on the *charpae* placed under a mosquito net on the roof. They were content even in their silence.

'Is it alarming that we are not talking?' asked Momina, snuggling next to Mehtab. 'We had plans of talking so much.'

'No, my love,' came a reply. 'We're accepting that we're finally one. How beautiful is that?'

'Indeed.'

'Also,' Mehtab smirked, 'I've been talking to you for the past twenty-five years, I think I have nothing to say anymore.'

Momina hit him playfully and rested her head on his shoulder. Mehtab had rather broad shoulders for a young man. 'I'm tired,' she said. 'Happy, sad, and tired.'

'Why are you sad, *meri jaan?*'

'Because of Laiba bhabhi.'

'Let's not talk about things we cannot control.'

Momina nodded and changed the top instantly. 'You look tired, too.'

'Of course, I just spent an hour taking pins out of your hair, it's like they stuffed the entire market in your head,' Mehtab laughed. The reflection of the moon could be seen in his eyes. He was all that Momina had ever wanted and that night, she knew that she would sleep like a newborn in her mother's lap – without a care in the world.

'Farz hai ab apka,' she said.

'Apke farz sar ankhoun per.'

And so, the lovers slept hand in hand, both facing each other, dreaming of different things. Momina, whose smile slowly turned upside down, and sweat wrapped the forehead, dreamt of being in a dark room screaming for Mehtab, and Mehtab, who seemed rather at peace, dreamt of floating in the clouds amongst people in capes.

Their life, as expected, was full of joy. Mehtab landed a job at the local police station, where he worked till noon, and then studied for the CSS examination that he had not managed to pass earlier. 'I was away from my Momina,' he said to Fouzia begum. 'Now that she's here, I will pass all my exams.' Momina spent all her time with Fouzia begum and her mother Shamila, and both the mothers taught her to differentiate between all *daals*, and how to cook them slowly.

'It's not the spices and the ingredients that make the most difference,' Shamila begum said. 'It's the *way* you cook it.'

Within a month, Momina could cook most of Mehtab's favorite dishes, and even though her food was far from what Fouzia begum made – Mehtab licked his fingers after having it, as if it was the very best in the world.

It wasn't as if the family had forgotten about Laiba. It was only that the rumor had flown that she had left Fouzia begum's eldest because there was only so much she could handle, and Zubair had even heard someone say that she went to her lover, and though that made Zubair tremble, a feeling he had only known when standing in front of the giant coolers, he had silently demanded the truth from his mother.

'We went after her,' Fouzia begum said. 'We did not find her. Her family is content with not telling us where she is. They-'

'They?'

'They just want her to be happy and they sent her to her extended family. They want to wait for some time and then they'll get back to us.'

'What about her dying dado?' asked Zubair - quickly digesting the first fact. If you were there, you'd say he took heartbreak like a gulp of water.

'She has been dead for years,' replied Fouzia begum silently. 'I'm sorry, beta.'

'It is fine. I would like that no one talk about it. At least not in front of me, and do not try to bring her back.'

'But...'

'Please.'

And after that day, no one mentioned Laiba, and Zubair came and went and sat and slept like he had never been married.

At this point in the story, I want you to sit down – wherever you can, but surely not on Fouzia begum's newly furnished sofa – it is for special guests, not that you aren't one, but we do not have her permission. Now that you've found a place to sit, I want you to breathe in and out, because what I am going to tell you is one of life's greatest tragedies, or as I would term it, life's horrid twists, and there's no ghee coating things like that.

On November 5th, six weeks after their marriage, when Momina burnt her *daal*, Fouzia begum had a severe pollen allergy after ten years, Zubair removed his wife's possessions from their shared cupboard, Mehtab Safi-ullah Saeed, the son of Riaz Safi-ullah Saeed, was hit by a train when crossing the road back home and was pronounced brain dead.

The news came as a shock as all horrible ones do – with the aftertaste of the *moong daal* under her tongue, Momina and Fouzia begum rushed to the hospital, where Zubair was already present. No one knew what had happened except that Mehtab was flown to the other side of the road by a cargo train because he was either willingly standing on the tracks or was pushed on them. The doctors, upon examining him and operating on him for eight hours, said that he was in a coma, but then later said that the blood loss had been too much, and now, he was brain dead and on artificial life support.

'It's all a joke,' Momina smiled, looking at her husband lying in bed. 'Mama jaan, there is no such thing as brain dead. You're either dead or not and Mehtab can never do that to me. L-look at him, dreaming like that. Dreaming of me.'

Fouzia begum collapsed in Shamila begum's arms, she could only hear her bahu's lips moving and no sound could be heard but the machinery functioning to keep her son breathing.

Chapter
3

When Momina had been young, her father had taken her to one of those Sunday festivals in the village that happened at the end of every month. This time, the festival was a rather grand one because the villagers had gotten together to arrange it. Momina vividly remembered the pink candy floss, having too much of it, the fries covered in ketchup – the artificial red of which did not wash out for days, and the train – the train that she sat on. She repeatedly wondered if it was the same train that had run over Mehtab. For some odd reason, she thought that she had been punished for having ridden the train too much, for not having given the other children turns. She had been a horrid child then, and this could have been a terrible comeback – but then she thought that the train should have hit her, not dear Mehtab, after all, he had to run the country one day, and he could not die so young.

The doctors did what they could, but Momina thought that it was not enough. They thought that if she could tell them how much she loved him, or that she too would die if they could not save him, the doctors would. But, alas, that did not happen. Mehtab's brain was dead, and his body was alive till Fouzia begum wanted it to be. Zubair, who for the very first time tasted salty tears and sweat curled up in the hospital washroom, had left the decision up to his mother, who wanted to get it over with. She had asked the doctor every hour of every day for one week if something could be done, but the answer had been no, and so looking at peaceful Mehtab lying on the bed, lingering between life and death, she thought to have him removed from artificial life support,. When Momina was informed, she threatened to end her life if such a decision was to be taken.

'A widow at such a young age, she's grieving. Let her have some time. In time, she will make the correct decision,' said the nurse to Fouzia begum.

And so, it was decided that Mehtab would be on life support till Momina would accept his death. And Momina, determined to bring him back to life, went to the hospital daily, soaked his drying blue body with a wet sponge and cloth, and brushed back what was left of his hair. The nurses looked at her in astonishment and said that she had gone insane in love, but also enjoyed every bit of Momina taking care of dead Mehtab as if this was what she was meant to do her entire life.

It was true that Momina was heartbroken and often people who're in such a state, lose their appetite and their hair and wander from one place to another like ghosts, but Momina was feeling something much more. Her head felt heavier, her feet were swollen up like balloons, and the smell of daal made her puke. Everything else she could digest – but daal made her tremble, vomit and faint.

'Daal reminds her of Mehtab, he loved it,' Fouzia begum said to the house help. 'We will no longer cook it, at least till my daughter gets well.'

But soon after, the water and the gobi started making Momina sick too and soon after Fouzia begum decided that no gobi would be cooked in the house, Momina stumbled down the stairs and landed on the carpeted lounge with a broken tooth. Troubled and deeply disturbed, Fouzia begum rushed her bahu to the hospital, stating that her daughter-in-law had gotten a terrible disease where she could not eat anything, but at the hospital it was found that Momina was pregnant with Mehtab's child. There was no denying it – the baby was there and it was the unborn that disliked daal and gobi.

Fouzia begum, who always wanted to become a dadi, felt the need to end her life at that moment. She thought: Momina was young, and her wedding had only lasted some months, and the child would grow up without a father like Mehtab and Zubair had, and Momina was no Fouzia begum – she could not face the hardships of life. She was a petite soul for whom an American style lighter was brought because she was afraid to light the stove with a matchstick.

Shamila begum knew that it was ill of her to even think the thought that she thought, asked Zubair if there could be a possibility of not having the child, and this very talk of hers, were carried by the thin walls to Momina who burst into tears and informed them that no one would take the life of the life inside her – it was the only living part of Mehtab, she had. Fouzia begum tried talking to Momina but her once obedient daughter-in-law had become stubborn, and she no longer listened to what Fouzia begum thought or wanted – it was her, a dead Mehtab and their child against the world.

'Nothing hurts me more than seeing her like this,' said Fouzia begum, 'but if she can act this way, I can too. I have lost my son and I wake up and I sleep. She can too. If she *wants* to keep us paying the hospital bills for Mehtab who is in pain because of her and if she *wants* to keep the child, then she cannot do it alone. She will have to be married soon after the child is born. If she can promise us that, we can promise her this.'

'You are right,' agreed Shamila begum. 'My heart aches for her but when we are no longer here, who will take care of her? Who will accept her with a child?'

'Someone will,' said Fouzia begum. 'That is for me to worry about.'

And so, Fouzia begum made it very clear to Momina – what the future held for her. Momina had listened and walked past the begum, without a care in the world.

'Do as you please,' she said under her breath. 'Find someone who can accept me and the child, for I am a burden for you all.'

After a few days, Fouzia begum made an announcement for two things – one, she wanted the finest cobbler to come and make shoes for Momina which would fit her swollen feet so that she would once again run around with sunshine on her cheeks. But Fouzia begum did not know that the cobbler's creation could not fix her broken Momina. Her second announcement was that she was on the hunt for a Rajput family, with a son no older than the age of thirty-five, who would accept a beautiful woman with a child to-be.

When the news got out, several women came to visit Fouzia begum with their sons. One of them, who had a factory nearby, brought their son on the very first meeting and it was evident that he could not take his eyes off of

Momina. He said that he would care for her and her son – he was too sure that it was a son, like his own. However, Fouzia begum was put off by his behavior and had them sent away.

'Fouzia begum,' said the mother of that man, 'there is nothing wrong with my son. He, at times, does not know what to say.'

'The boy who marries my bahu,' came the reply, 'should always know what to say. She is a gem, and a gem cannot be given to someone who speaks before he thinks.'

The woman, furious as ever, answered in quite a lady-like manner, 'If that is the case, then the news has reached us that the wife of your eldest son, who you have brought up, has left. Why do you not wed off your precious gem to him?'

For the very first time in life, Fouzia begum was left dumbfounded and did not know what to say and so she said nothing. 'Why do I not wed Momina to Zubair?' she gasped to herself. 'He will accept the child like no one else will.'

Fouzia begum ran to Shamila begum, and told her about what had just happened and Shamila begum burst into tears, saying that she had been waiting to hear that and so, both of them went up to Zubair, and told him what they thought.

'If you have decided it,' said Zubair, 'I will have no problem accepting it. You know better. But it is only fair that I tell you, that Laiba has left me but not my heart, and it is a possibility that she might never leave it but I can promise that I will take care of Momina like Mehtab would have.'

Fouzia begum beamed in delight. That day, a lot of things were happening for the very first time. For instance, her face lit up and she was more proud of Zubair than she had ever been.

'Zubair bhai?' Momina said, without reacting to the news of her future, like the women thought she would. 'You want me to marry a man I think of as a brother, who is in love with another woman?'

'It is nonsense. He will love you and it is only him who will love you and your child,' said Shamila begum. 'All my life I have listened to you and this time, you have to listen to me. That is all your old mother asks of you.'

Momina strolled across the room in her leather shoes – though her heart was sinking, her feet felt the most comfortable they had in ages. She no longer cared what happened to her, for losing Mehtab had meant losing her life, and now, everything was the same – meaningless.

'But Islam says that I cannot be married whilst I'm still married,' she said, trying to make her case, knowing very well that the begums would have an answer for her.

'The papers will be ready by tomorrow,' said Fouiza begum. 'You will sign, then you will no longer be Mehtab's wife. Islam also says that you cannot be married till the child will be delivered. So before that, only a small engagement will be done. A 'haan' function, telling the world that you are Mrs. Zubair.'

'I will not sign any paper. Mehtab is dead, I am already a widow.'

'He is not legally, for you have my son on life support. He lives and dies every second.' said Fouzia begum, and then left the room. Shamila begum went after her, thinking that her daughter had upset her dear sister, and Momina stood alone, smiling at the walls.

'These are the walls Laiba bhabhi ran away from,' she said to herself. 'And now I know why she did. But I am content,' she assured herself. 'Zubair bhai will not expect anything of me, and it is better to have him, than a man I have to please.'

After two months, a small ceremony was set in the garden of the house. The trees that were months ago lit, now drooped low and had shed their leaves - it was as if they too grieved, and Fouzia begum wore the same *khussas* she had worn on Mehtab and Momina's wedding – in which she danced her heart out, but now, she could barely walk in them.

Only a few people were called. After the ceremony, fish was served. Momina, who trembled at the sight of Zubair, and the cut up fish, felt nauseated and as soon as the ring exchange *rasam* was done, fled from the gathering to her room.

'I do not know what upsets me more,' she cried, pressing her stomach. 'His face, or the fish.'

After the engagement, nothing changed, except that Momina's stomach grew bigger, and a few gifts from relatives came in, some for her and some for Zubair. She paid no heed to them and asked Fouzia begum if she could go to Lahore to start buying things for the baby.

'We do not know the gender,' Fouzia begum said. 'I will accompany you and buy the best new, modern things I can for my grandson. But for now, you must rest. Unless, you want to go with Zubair.' Momina chose to rest.

On the ninth of June, when the weather was rather sunny and the announcement of Ramadan starting the next day had been made in the mosques, Zubair received a call from the hospital. He was expecting it to be for the bill that was due for his brother's machine, but it was the nurse shouting at the end of the other line, that God had visited the hospital that night – that a miracle had happened: Mehtab had woken up.

Everyone rushed to the hospital, and Momina, on her way there, threw the diamond ring on her finger in one of the street's bins that the government had recently placed.

Upon reaching, they were told to wait as the doctor was inside, examining the patient.

'There can be some trouble remembering or not knowing what has happened all this time,' he told Zubair. 'But I will pray namaz and so should you, as this is a miracle.'

Before anything could be said or done, the doctor lined everyone up in a queue, and pointed towards the crying faces, asking a rather anorexic looking – *gutli* of a mango-like Mehtab, to name everyone.

'Mama,' he said. 'Shamila aunty,' he said. 'Zubair.'

'And who is Zubair?'

'My bhai.'

'And what about her?' asked the doctor, pointing at Momina who stood there jumping on the side of the bed with her stomach covered with a chiffon scarf.

'Momina.'

'And who is Momina?'

'My little cousin.'

Fouzia begum placed her hand on her son's wrinkled skin. He seemed as if he had aged rapidly. His face looked like a *khajoor*.

'Momina…' she said to him. 'Is pregnant.'

'Yes,' Mehtab replied. 'MashAllah, Momina. You did not tell me. I don't seem to remember your marriage. I…'

'Please don't pressure the patient into remembering if he doesn't,' the doctor cut in.

'Zubair,' Fouzia begum said at once. 'He's the father. Momina is his wife.'

'Oh,' Mehtab cut in. 'MashAllah bhai, yes. I cannot wait.'

Momina collapsed onto the floor, and if her heart had not been broken before, this time, it splattered into little pieces, way out of her reach, and she begged during her long breaths, for Allah to take her at that very moment.

'Bhabhi needs help,' Mehtab said, gulping down his fourth glass of water.

37

Chapter
4

When Momina turned twenty, she rented her first-ever videotape and saw a movie whose name she did not remember. She had to hide the videotape in the stack of other videotapes, so she ripped the cover off and even though she knew the name of the characters in the movie, she did not know what the movie was called. In that movie, a woman who was tied up by kidnappers, saw the bad men shooting her little girl at a distance and the woman was fully awake but she was completely hopeless and could do nothing to help the girl. The English woman stood there, tears streaming down her face, groaning in agony – seeing her child die.

That is precisely how Momina felt – unlike the woman, she could move, she could talk, she could see Mehtab waking up, sleeping, and sitting next to her every day, and yet, Momina could only scream inside, as he sat right beside her, without a care in the world. She wondered if it would have been easier with him being dead.

'Salam, bhabhi,' he said and offered her sweet toast that Zubair had gotten from the city. Mehtab did remember to have toast with the sides cut and *makhan* only on the edges, he made sure the massi made it that way – so specific he was about the details, but he did not remember his Momina – the woman he had loved his entire life.

During this time, Zubair could sense Momina's helplessness. He could see the plea for help in her eyes, and after having loved Laiba, he could imagine how terrible it felt. And so, he went up to talk to his mother – begum Fouzia, to free Momina of this captivity.

'It is horrible to see her like this,' Zubair said. 'I cannot help hearing her sobs at night.'

'Those sobs are for Mehtab not remembering her, not for being engaged to you,' came the reply.

'Even if you leave her, which as my son you will not, it is not like Mehtab can marry her. He thinks of her as nothing but his brother's wife,' she continued.

'I do not know what to do,' said Zubair. 'It is not just that, I do not feel for her.'

Fouzia Begum took a pause and then looked at her son. Zubair looked tired after a long day of surgery, and his face was unshaven, and deep down, she knew that he was hung up on his first wife, who he had refused to divorce. So, she did what she had been always doing her entire life – planning for her children, and making sure that the plans worked as they did in her head.

'The radio base station was shut for some days and so Shamila's telephone had no signals, but she had gotten the news from Laiba's family. They are sending the papers for *khula*.'

Zubair looked at his mother. He had known her a long time to realize that the tip of her nose turned pink when she lied, which she often did and so, he said what she wanted to hear.

'I will try to be a better husband to Momina.'

Fouzia begum was a lady of much intelligence, and thinking that she had done a horrid deed, having married a woman who truly loved her youngest to her eldest, haunted her. But she had prayed to God to help, and God had washed away Mehtab's memory – and to her, that was assurance.

Two things happened simultaneously during this time: First, Zubair, abiding by the promise he had made to his mother, and also to himself to not miss Laiba, a woman he had given his heart to, started appreciating the little things Momina did – from packing his tiffin even if it was a duty she did out of responsibility and not love, running to the washer with his clothes, in her free time asking about how awful it is that he has to cut up people for a living, and then ending it by always saying that if she was to die, he shouldn't slaughter her under any cost. Zubair knew that Momina did not love him, he understood that she might never do, but he liked how amidst a broken heart, she put up an act for him and the others.

The second thing was that even though Momina was proving to be a good wife-to-be to the eye, as she was taught by Shamila begum, under her dupatta was hidden a secret; she was fixated on winning back Mehtab – proving that she had truly loved and so whilst she ran with Zubair's clothes, she stopped to sniff Mehtab's and as she sat with Zubair asking him about his day, she wondered if he would mention his younger brother, and all the things in Zubair's tiffin were Mehtab's favorite.

As her stomach grew, so did her anxiety. Momina stayed up nights wondering of things she could do to make Mehtab remember her before the baby could be born and before she would be wedded to Zubair. But, she made the grave mistake of not realizing that she was not the only one up at night. One day, Momina took out a black box, wrapped in purple velvet, and out of it came an emerald green earring. This piece of jewelry held a special place in her heart for Mehtab had gifted it to her years ago and she had worn it year after year, till once, when they had been sitting under the shade of a banyan tree, and when Mehtab had pecked her neck, the earring had fallen somewhere between the dispersed autumn leaves, and the next day they had not been able to find it. So Momina kept that one earring that she had, closed in a box, tucked away in her closet. She was sure that the glittery ornament would make *him* remember – if not all, the kiss, that afternoon and her.

She went into his room when he was out for fajr prayer, something that he had only started doing after getting well, and placed the looped earring under his pillow. She wanted to stand there and breathe in his odor, but careful to not get caught, she ran out. Had she stayed, she would have stood a better chance of escaping Fouzia begum's eyes, who was right outside the door and watched her *bahu* scamper off to the kitchen. Alarmed, but clearly intact, Fouzia begum went inside. Her worst fear was that Mehtab had been told everything, but he wasn't home so Fouzia begum swept across the room, looking for signs of a voodoo doll – a very *aam* occurrence at her time, to get the lover back. She ended up finding the green emerald earring and clutching it tightly in her hand, she walked out.

Fouzia begum thought a long time about what should be done and she thought very hard after which one day she went quietly into Mehtab's room, closed the door and talked to him about something – and since the door was closed, we did not hear what was being said, but there was a tear or two, and from the window, we could see that she had held her son's hand. Mehtab was quiet at first - as if he too was thinking – something Fouzia begum had been immersed in the past week, and then he placed his hand back on his mother's – which seemed much like an agreement.

That afternoon, accompanied by a few women, but not Shamila begum, Fouzia begum in her white dress, rode off to the village side. Momina noticed how dressed her mother-in-law was, and how many presents were inside the suitcases – big and small, fancy and unwrapped, all sorts of them. And the kitchen of Uncle ZumZum across the street smelled like milk Ladoos, and so she asked her mother what all that was about. Shamila begum knew nothing, and neither did Zubair, and so, Momina went to Mehtab and asked him about it. 'It is very unlikely for bari mama to not tell us something,' she said. 'Do you know?' Momina wanted to continue her speech and ask about the earring – mainly because Mehtab was not making eye contact and acting hesitant – but she repeated what she had asked earlier. 'If you do not know, you can tell me. And if you *do* know, pray tell me.'

Mehtab looked at Momina and smiled. Her face lit up like a Christmas tree, like the flat in the building of Muslims in Ramadan at 3am – her face lit up like the bulb hanging above them.

'It's a surprise,' Mehtab said. 'Ama is off to make things right, but till then, I cannot talk.'

Momina examined him from head to toe. She thought that her plan had worked: Mehtab had found the earring, remembered everything or at least some of it, confronted his mother, and now Fouzia begum was on his way to fetch Laiba, and by night time or the next day – all would be well. Suddenly, Momina did not despise her swollen stomach anymore, or the fact that Mehtab had left the room. She felt her nerves relax, and just there, on the living room sofa, Momina fell into a deep and most peaceful slumber.

At night, Fouzia begum returned with numerous unfamiliar faces, and she collected everyone from her family, even Shamila begum, and with utter joy, asked Mehtab to step forward, whilst a woman came from behind her, dressed in a white dress similar to that of Fouzia begum's.

'This,' said Fouzia begum, 'is Kiran. She's the daughter of a city merchant in Lahore and all her siblings are married and I am thankful for her parents for giving me the hand for their darling woman, who was not short of men waiting to marry her. But she is going to be the wife of my Mehtab.'

Mehtab laughed and held Kiran's hand – Fouzia begum almost frowned as it was too early to do so, but seeing that Momina was standing in the corner, watching with an expressionless face, she too rejoiced with the others. Shamila begum clapped, but deep down, her heart felt heavy for she knew that her daughter was still hung up on the hope of the now groom-to-be.

Fouzia begum brought Momina forward and introduced everyone to her, and their unborn grandchild, and quoted how Zubair was very fond of her, and Momina forced a smile – the lights and the people, all appearing fuzzy to her, except Mehtab, who she could make out even with watery eyes and a broken heart. That night, as Momina wept in her mother's arms, Shamila begum wept with her, but then, said what she should have told her daughter months back.

'Life is unfair, it has been unfair to Fouzia begum as the man she loved left her for another woman – got bored of her. It has been unfair to me for I lost my son when you were nine. It has been unfair to all men and women and now it is testing you. But my daughter, what is fair and what is unfair? Only you get to decide that. It has taken from you but it has given to you, as well. For others, it just takes, works halfway. And if you accept it, it will give you more and more. Much more than now. I can see that Zubair has accepted you and one day he will love you but if you do not…'

'I cannot love him back.'

'Maybe, but you can accept him. That's the first step.'

After a week, a tremendously long week for both Begum Fouzia and Momina, Momina went into labor and delivered a healthy baby girl, and the very first thing the surrounding people said was how beautiful she was, and how much she resembled her *chacha*.

After 5 Years

Outside a school, sat comfortably in Zubair's newly purchased vehicle, his wife Momina and he-himself, under the scorching sun, waiting for Mehrose to come. Zubair tucked away the strand of hair sticking to his wife's sweaty forehead behind her ear and though Momina fidgeted, she smiled. He then asked her if she wanted street corn, something he had never been fond of, having studied germs, but it was all worth it as Momina's face lit up. 'With lemon and masala!' she said.

* * *

Inside a room, sat Mehtab with his desk drawer open, and placed under the newspaper and medicine strips was the green earring. He looked at it, and he was once again teleported to the noon under the tree with the woman he had so fondly loved. In all truth, he had never forgotten, but being told about what had been done when he had been fast asleep and almost on his way to God, he did not blame anyone – and for him, his brother's happiness mattered the most. And so, these little moments of feeling that day's wind, and the coconut lotion on her neck, were enough to last a lifetime.

'Are you ready, *jaan?*'

Mehtab quickly placed the earring away and snapped back to his senses. 'Jee Kiran, just a moment.'

The Never Happening Shaadi of Shaazia Farooq

The Iqbals never called back. Aba was very sure that they would, since their Araein son was persistent on marrying a Rajput from Lahore, because he considered the blood royal. Even his Ami didn't mind that I wore spectacles and refused to get laser. 'Dekahin,' I told her, 'Even if I get it, your son is short-sighted and so am I, so our child might be a *chashmish,* my laser won't change that.' They loved how my silky hair touched my knees, and how I made the most delicious cardamom tea with a hint of ginger, and that I did not mind giving up my job to be a housewife, since I never had been the studious kind and the marketing degree was hardly doing me any good. But, even then, the Iqbals – a rather mediocre family with three sons – two of whome had married out of love and brought home rather sharp *bahus,* did not call Aba back. For some time, Ama assumed that they didn't have credit, as she often ran out of it, and also because they weren't as well off as us, but when three weeks passed, we were sure that it wasn't the case.

This was the thirteenth family who had rejected me and we had no clue why. Aba had money, lots of it, and I had a plot in Bahria Town to my name, not that we were any fan of *jahez,* but that wasn't the issue. I was twenty-eight, and my elder sisters had all been married before they turned twenty-five, and truth be told, I was much taller, prettier, and more shaadi-material than any of them. I was an already ripe fruit, with a noticeable white hair strand that made Ama lose sleep on most nights. My elder sister, a mother of two, who was more interested in marrying me off than the schooling of her spoiled daughters, thought that my chachy had done some *ilm* on me as chachy's daughters were corpulent and dark, and we weren't, she was envious. Apa had, at one time, even found some *taweez* under my bed, signifying that it was all due to black magic. A part of me wanted to believe that, because it made me feel better about myself – the fact that it was the universe at work, and not my recently acne-prone skin.

The fourteenth family that visited me just before the virus arrived in Pakistan, changed my life. The family was small, a rather sweet Ami, a *nand* that hardly spoke, and a well-groomed, graduated-from-an-Australian-university son. In fact, the *rishta* was too good to be true. On learning about two broken engagements of mine, aunty laughed it off. She said that even though Musa was her only son, she wanted me to shift to Australia with him right after marriage. She wanted no lavish function and no dowry, and in case we wanted a grand function, *they* wanted to pay for it. It almost felt as if it was a staged joke but aunty assured us that it was not. Aba, however, was not bought. He felt that something was terribly off but Ama, on the other hand, brushed it off, saying that this was the *rishta* that had to happen all along. Truth be told, I felt it too – the connection, the sudden spark, the feeling of undigested samosas in my lower stomach. Musa wasn't very good-looking, especially since he had recently gotten bald, but his caramel brown eyes locked into mine and his smile -supporting dimples- made my legs wobble, and mind you, I wasn't even standing. At that moment, Aba, Ama, and aunty disappeared, it was him and me, looking at each other, with an assurance that this was it.

Aunty followed up the very next day, and the day after that came with *shagun:* homemade *mithai* with brightly colored clothes, neatly packed with ribbons and bangles, and of course, a note from Musa, "Cannot wait, my dear Shaazia. Till we cannot meet, we shall meet, in sleep." I thought that it was romantic but Aba cringed. He did not even look at the gifts. Later that night, something weird happened – so much so that I cannot explain it, at least I could not at that time. I slept after dinner and dreamt that I was standing outside a huge, but rather unkempt villa, and the doors opened as I went forward. Somehow, I knew my way around, I knew where the cats were asleep, where I had to tip-toe because the family was asleep, and most of all – I knew where Musa was. When I reached his room, the door did not automatically open, in fact, I pushed it with all my might, and there, right behind it, stood Musa, smiling at me.

"I do not understand," I said, when I saw him. "H-How am I here?"

"It is a dream," he replied. He signaled me to sit down on a moving cloud near his window or it might have been a cushion, but it was as soft as a cloud.

"It feels very real."

"Dreams are but the reality, the reality when our eyes are closed, my love. I knew from the moment that I saw you, you'd make it till the door."

"I-I don't understand."

"I have loved before," said Musa, "but nothing quite like ours. And no one could meet me in my dream and that's how I knew *she* wasn't the one."

That was our very first meeting. It continued every night, sometimes even at noon, and I looked forward to sleeping. We mostly sat in the room, but sometimes we roamed around the streets of Model Town. No human could notice us and we stole fresh orange juices – but at times, the street dogs stared at us and barked. Even without meeting Musa, I was meeting him and falling deeply in love.

A few weeks passed, and Aba came home one night, flushed with happiness, and we thought that we had won the lottery as he had always invested in bonds and tickets and anything that could be scratched. He even kept old phone cards, thinking that after a year the number could be repeated and entered again for balance. That was classic Aba.

"We *have* won the lottery," he said, his eyes gleaming with joy. "But better than anything. My brother Yawar is finally returning from Scotland."

"I thought Yawar chacha was in Ireland."

"Yes, yes, whatever land he is in! He is coming to Pakistan for the first time in twenty-five years, and even before landing, he had expressed his wish for Abdur-Rehman, his one and only, successful son, our blood, to be married to Shaazia!"

Ama was even more ecstatic than Aba. Yawar chacha was loaded, in both education and money, and for the longest time, many in our family had inquired about his son. For a moment, I smiled too, but then, right after, I remembered Musa, and our daily meetings, and I realized that I could not imagine not having them – not having

Musa in my life anymore.

I talked to Ama about not knowing Yawar chacha's son properly, about how men raised abroad have forgotten traditional values, and about the retardation rate of children in cousin marriages.

"Your Aba and I are cousins and you turned out just fine, so don't give me this new world science."

Of course, I couldn't tell them that I had grown fond of Musa – they had only met him once, and I certainly could not break Aba's trust. That night, I slept with a heavy heart.

As I swept between sleep and wakefulness, I arrived where the sky was a shade darker, and the roads emptier and I found myself outside of Musa's house. He crept from behind, holding a carrot.

"I love eating carrots in dreams, my love. They taste so much better than they do in reality. The crunch, the tip-"

He examined my silence from head to toe. "What is it that worries you?"

"I-nothing," I replied.

"The sun is not shining and the wind is rather cold."

"So?"

"You've brought it with you. Your feelings. Tell me, *meri jaan,* so I can make it better."

I looked at him. His reassuring smile stretching to form a dimple, and his spectacles almost sliding off his sharp nose - I stepped forward and hugged him. I wanted to know what it felt like to hug someone in a dream - to hug Musa - and it felt warm, much like all of my birthdays come at once. Musa's hands slid up my chest and he pulled me even closer, till all I could sniff was his skin and the faint odor of Safeguard soap.

"What's wrong," he asked again. He sat me down and

held my hand.

"Do you mind me doing that?"

I shook my head, and pressed my fingers between his.

"Tell me, what's wrong?"

And so, I told him what was happening. I told him about how Aba never liked him from the start and thought that everything was too good to be true. I told him about chacha Yawar and then, after a deep sigh, I told him about my marriage being set up with a cousin I had never seen.

Musa laughed. "That's all?" he asked. "That's the problem?"

"Y-yes, but why are you laughing? It's serious. And I don't want to marry him!"

"Why don't you want to marry him?"

"Because I don't want to lose you," I replied.

"Well, you won't."

The sky became a shade lighter, and the sun started peeking from behind the clouds. I felt better.

"You see, my dear Shaazia, your Aba is somewhat right," said Musa. "He must have thought why a man like me hadn't been married, or why my mother was offering a lot. It's because, Shaazia, I sleep a lot. I sleep in the morning, noon and night."

"But you were awake when you came and met us," I interrupted.

He swung his arm around my shoulder and I felt my stomach churn – the good kind when you're having too much to eat, and you know it, but it's worth the aftermath.

"I do wake up, after two days or so, sometimes after five. My body will die if I do not but it is not the real-life that I enjoy, it is this. I am almost always here, living the life of my dreams, in my dreams, and no matter what time you come, your Musa is here."

"Oh - so if we had married, I would have to sleep the entire day too?"

"I wouldn't have forced you, but yes. You see, *iss liye* Ama wanted to give you the world. To put up with me."

"You're amazing. Y-you're not that difficult to put up with."

Musa looked at me. He then brushed back my hair and there from behind my back appeared some corn. "You were in the mood for it, were you not?" he said.

"How did you know?"

"When you've been asleep this long, it is easy to interpret others' dreams. You, my simple darling soul, wanted some corn, the type you had eaten in Murree, with some lemon on top."

Before my very eyes appeared a lemon, and Musa squeezed it on top of the corn.

"It can taste better than Murree's, it can taste like the best corn in the world," he continued. "You just have to imagine it."

And so, Musa and I sat, looking at whatever we wanted, hand in hand, promising each other that no matter what happened, nothing could separate us.

Two months later, I got married to my cousin. He was nothing like Musa and he hardly slept. I was unhappy and heartbroken, but Musa had whispered in my ear that I was the luckiest in the world – I had managed to keep my parents happy *and* be with the love of my life, and there was no denying that. And on the first night of my marriage with Abdur-Rehman, I slept early and made love to Musa. I was indeed guilt-stricken, but it felt right and it was a dream I never wanted to wake up from.

As time passed, and I bonded with my cousin-husband, I realized that I did not love him, but I did feel terrible cheating on him, with whatever it was that I did.

I ended up talking to a psychologist, who said that all this was not possible, but only a fragment of my imagination because I was running away from the feelings I had developed for a stranger - Musa. She made me believe that it was alright and that none of it was real. Sometime later, when I missed my period, I learned that I was expecting. This was when I started feeling closer to Rehman more than ever, and he too made sure that I felt loved and cared for. I understood that Musa did all that he could in a blink of an eye, because he had access to my dreams and wants, but Rehman had started making the effort for it. During this time, I got as little sleep as possible, because even though I could not help standing outside Musa's house, I no longer wanted it. Truth be told, I was scared of letting him go and even more frightened of not having my husband in my life. It was as if I could not choose between night and day. I loved Musa, I knew I did, but my body no longer craved his existence, in fact, it repelled it because unlike me, it could tell right from wrong.

The psychologist said that in time, all would be well. This child would bring me and my husband together and that's what I aimed for. Musa knew that I was expecting, and instead of asking any questions, he made sure that I always met him in a cornfield, surrounded by all things happy. I knew that he could feel me being distant, but he answered it with love and well, corn. In my second trimester, during a rather casual talk, my gynecologist said that I should catch up on sleep because as astonishing as it was for her, my baby was developing only when I slept – and that is when it dawned upon me, that Musa was here to stay.

The Jinn in Majhbeen's Phupho

Five friends.
One dark secret.
A haunting day to remember...

Chapter
1

The Mutton and the Mosquito

"I don't want to make mutton for them," Hira scoffed. "In fact, I don't even want to meet them."

Farhan rubbed his beard which had been unshaven since the partial lockdown. He then got up, rolled his eyes at his wife and left the room – all whilst itching the curls falling off the tip of his chin.

"Haan, fine," Hira continued. "Walk off like that. I'll go to *ami's* house for Qa week if this continues. It's better than putting up with your demands!"

Farhan and Hira were *that* couple – you know, the picture-perfect kind, who make all aunties go *haw* because of their love marriage. They'd been with each other for six years, but they preferred to say three because that's how long they had been married. The fights were a routine and now that they were forcefully put together under one roof, the frequency of the brawls had increased. Hira's ami had always instructed her to marry a man who liked her biryani.

"He hates rice. He hates *biryani*. Who hates *biryani* and most importantly who hates *my biryani?*"

"Come on *ami*, you're overreacting. So what if he doesn't like *biryani?*"

"Beta, the debate is always about who likes it with *aloo* and who likes it without it. Never about who doesn't like it at all. If he can't appreciate a bowl of spicy *chawal,* he certainly can't appreciate you."

Hira never deciphered whether her mother was joking. She had ultimately thought that it was a harmless *muzaak* but then on their *haan* function, her *ami* had ended up ordering two types of biryani and had forced her *damad* to finish a plate. Despite her mother's constant hilarious attempts to belittle the husband-to-be's family, the *shaadi* date was set and with little *dhoom dhaam* that mediocre families could afford, the couple was wedded.

* * *

Brushing away the curls sticking to her forehead, Hira scampered after Farhan. She was a hyper woman for her age, filled with raging emotions, un-said gossip and the undying belief of ending up husband-less if she ever let Farhan sleep with a fight.

She spotted her husband lighting a piece of paper, an odd thing he often did, perhaps to overcome the need to smoke again- and twitching her artificially turned peach nose in the air, Hira went up to him.

"Acha na. Stop this. I've had time to think. You can invite them over but no mutton, *theek hai?*"

Farhan turned around and smiled. "We can order the mutton chops but there has to be mutton. You know how particular Mohsin *wagera* are about it. We're meeting after a long time, let's put the *purani baatein* aside."

The sun had set and the couple sat in the balcony, looking at the empty roads and birds circling the sky. Both of them knew what had happened five years back but none of them dared speak about it. They were content with the mutton worries.

"Will all of them *really* come?" Hira asked, breaking the silence.

"I don't know. I hope they will." came a reply.

* * *

Majhbeen loosely tied her hair in a bun and placed the scarf on her head. "Aunty, I'm going to offer *namaz*. If you need anything please wait."

Her aunty nodded and out of courtesy which she seldom showed to her daughter-in-law, lowered the sound of the television drama. The old age had gotten to her and she thought that Majhbeen deliberately started her prayer when the climax scene was to arrive. *"Aidhi tu naek,"* she muttered under her medicine breath.

As a young child, Majhbeen had always dreamed of being married to an army officer. None of her family members were in the army, but those early PTV shows with handsome looking men being greeted everywhere rejoiced in her mind. She was also one of those children who when asked what they wanted to be as grownups, blushed and said *dulhan* without a second thought. Her noticeable feature was the dimple on her left cheek which added volume to her otherwise plain face. And with such ordinary features, she assumed she'd never score a charming man dressed in a uniform. However, her *khala* had a friend whose brother had a best friend who was in the navy, and he wasn't that good-looking but he had received an award or two and there were promising rumors of him being promoted to a high rank within the circle. So one day her *khala* proposed the *rishta* to Majhbeen's mama whilst Majhbeen was busy making tea. When the match was made, Majhbeen was informed and it was pretended like she had a say in what had happened.

Rashid was a boring man and the problem with boring men is that their lives can never be spontaneous. It's always the same chair they seat themselves on, and the same color they adore and the same movie scene they laugh to, and with their in-built lifelong *boriat,* comes loyalty that they forever flaunt. Majhbeen had been married to him for a year and she had learned his likes and dislikes within the first week. As for Rashid, getting to know Majhbeen didn't matter. What mattered was having an understanding wife that nodded even in her sleep.

After the first week of marriage, Rashid left for work and only came back for some days at the end of the month. Majhbeen was married to Rashid's mother and it was she who decided what Rashid gave to Majhbeen or when he went to his room at night to sleep and absolutely nothing could be done about it.

* * *

"Aunty, do you need anything?" Majhbeen inquired, folding the prayer mat.

"Have you washed the dishes? Rubina is not coming. You can leave them for tomorrow morning if you want, *awein phir Rashid ko btao gi,"* aunty replied.

"I'll wash the dishes," Majhbeen answered after a pause. "And I don't tell Rashid anything."

"Bilkul."

Majhbeen couldn't help but notice the dirt under

her mother-in-law's chin. There was an evident layer that she had the urge to scrub off. Even around her butterfly-like nostrils that expanded in anger, a cluster of ingrown hair had marked their territory. Aunty looked back at her, and Majhbeen quickly looked elsewhere, gulped and hesitantly walked to the door.

"Aunty," she said. "I have to meet my friends tomorrow. *Idhar pass main hi,* in Gulberg. We'll have lunch *Hira kay ghar per* and just do *gup shap.* I thought I'd-"

"*Haan, haan. Chali jana. Yeh Hira koun hai.* But you won't get the driver. He has to wash the curtains. Go *Uber per.* And *wesay bhi,* they're closing the roads these days. *Wapsi atta leti ana.*"

Majhbeen was always reluctant to talk to her mother-in-law. In just one breath, she could instruct a thousand things and give a thousand *taane* and sometimes even make her repeat what she had said. So before the *saas* could remember anything else that they were going to run out of, or most importantly before she could ask if Majhbeen had gotten Rashid's permission, or if there would be any *londay* at the lunch, Majhbeen hurried out of the room.

* * *

Miles away from Hira, Farhan and Majhbeen sat with two of their long-lost friends, Zaryab and Mohsin-brothers who were finishing off some construction work in Lahore. Not twins, but very alike looking, the boys had been the talk of the town – or at least LSE, for four long years. There was nothing peculiarly great about them, but they looked good in Lahore's heat, and their jawlines were like geometrical shapes, and their baggy clothes imported from countries whose names only they could pronounce.

They had a large group of friends, social as they were, but closest to them had been Hira, Farhan, and Majhbeen. They had met like most friends meet, during a group project on a rather tedious day, and suddenly they had jokes amongst themselves.

"Are we up for tomorrow?" Zaryab inquired, puffing a dense Iraqi cigar. "Tastes like cardboard. *Wapsi per Gold Leaf ki dandi pakar lena.*"

He was initially answered in silence as Mohsin examined the shades of the sky. He had always been the artistic one, stuck in his father's business dream, making doodles on the backside of management notes. *"Haan.* It's been too long. *Jo hou gya so hou gya.* Let's go, meet them, congratulate them, have good food and head back home. Lahore has too many mosquitos anyway."

It wasn't the *machar* Mohsin disliked, it was the thought of being in the same city that the event had taken place that petrified him.

The five of them had spent strings of afternoons together doing nothing and had called each other home, and now, it wasn't like the brothers had more important things to do; like build tall buildings – it's just that the past sent shivers down their spine and meeting *them* meant reliving the past.

Chapter
2

The Eid of 2015

The curtains had been dusted clean but the shadiness of the cloth still made them look old. Hira had always thought that a new life meant a new house and a new everything. The house was an apartment and it had come with a decent balcony, but the walls that held it together felt like they would collapse any second. Coated with layers of matte paint, and furnished with lighting that illuminated her husband's choice of color – they still looked sad. If that wasn't enough, the worn-out *samaan* from Farhan's house had been handed to them for a new beginning.

"Old is *never* gold. Old is bloody old," Hira muttered under her breath as she sliced the cucumbers into perfect squares.

Hira Naeem had been born in a house where money was spent on acquired etiquettes and showoff, where the painting in the lounge was shown with its price being quoted to every *mehmaan,* but the Rooh-afza in the glass was measured.

"But ami it's not sweet," Hira had said.

"Neither is that *Shameem* sitting in the lounge. The trick is to add some sugar and use less syrup."

Hira's personality was a little of everything. She was snobby, but she never meant to be and she was selfish, but it was only for her and Farhan and a child she soon wanted to come. And though she was a soul who squashed hand-sized Lahori lizards with her Bata slippers, quite recently her heart had started beating fast, perhaps with fear. As the knife hit the cutting board, her fingers trembled. The sound of the continuous chopping waved her thoughts back to the *chand raat,* five years ago.

* * *

2015

"Stop moving! You'll get the mehndi on your new dress!" exclaimed a younger-looking Majhbeen. Behind her wriggling braid stuffed with fancy pins, sat a chubby Hira – plump cheeks, hazel lenses, and an out of fashion, shimmering red dress.

"You're taking too long," Hira exclaimed. "It'll take ages to dry and the function is at 8!"

"Today's Eid. Everyone will come late. My family distributes eidi after dinner and no one's coming to phupho *ki shaadi* empty handed."

The girls sat, hand in hand, giggling over who would look better in the color-coordinated dressing; the brothers or Farhan. The answer to that, as both of them knew, wasn't the latter but that's what happens in love, your man, no matter how unpleasant looking, is your knight in shining armor.

The room was full of aunties and uncles and little Gujrati girls who looked like aunties with heaped on makeup and artificial jewelry. Majhbeen didn't mind that her family was *paindu.* She adored each one of them. She adored her phupho the most, who was, without any doubt, a second mama to her. Who had fed her milk when her own child had died. And that day, Majhbeen was the happiest, for her phupho was finally getting married to a great man. The subtle whispering of the men and the curious eyes of the women in the room didn't bother her. She knew that they were aware of phupho's story and they were waiting, desperately, to be part of a ceremony that had never worked out in the past.

Hira loved Majhbeen's phupho as well - the kind of admiration you have for an unknown person with a tragic life. She knew that what had happened was not phupho's fault and the fact that she had lived her life with so much bravery had made Hira believe that good phuphos did exist in this world after all.

As the chitter and chatter grew intense, and the room became more crowded, a woman dressed in faded brown, with a hint of maroon akin to a rose blooming out of mud, entered the room. Her tired eyes stretched across her face with contentment, and a peachy-pink lipstick was smeared on her lips in an attempt to subtract years out of her age. She was older than many other women in the room, but the way she hopped from one corner to the next was a surety of her heart being that of a child's.

"Phupho jaan," Majhbeen exclaimed. "You look ravishing."

"Ravishing?" Hira cut in. "She looks like a star."

The girls gathered around the bride and sang joyous songs.

The sounds of *dholak* echoed outside the house as

Hira excused herself from the festivities to check up on her lover. She spotted Farhan some yards away, standing under the blinking lamppost, with a few other men in the street, where the wind was calmer. It was funny how a few steps had transformed Hira's surroundings from the singing wind to a cold, restless breeze knocking on the *dulhaan's* door. The men of the family had not yet entered as they were waiting for the *baraat,* and Farhan stood with them, not to welcome the groom, but to kiss some sweet tobacco.

"What's taking them so long?" Hira asked, whirling her *lehnga* next to Farhan.

"McDonald's *ruke huwe hai.*"

"Hain?"

"Oh *nae yaar.* I don't know where they are. Probably on their way. *Eid ki waja say rush bhi tou hai na.* Acha, you go inside. All the uncles are looking at you. *Shabash,* off you go."

Hira *did* understand Farhan's sarcasm but she always pretended not to, because she felt it made her appear adorable in front of him. And she very much enjoyed being told off – well, because it was Farhan after all.

＊ ＊ ＊

"Jaan!"

Hira's thoughts were disrupted by her husband walking in the kitchen. "How long till everything gets done?"

"Oh- well," Hira answered, pushing away the five-year-old memory, "The lasagna is in the oven, the order for *naan* is given. You have to fetch the mutton-chops, and uh - the Chinese will be ready in an hour."

"Mutton *abhi lay aoun?*"

"Of course not. It'll get cold even in the hotpot. Rush *hai, tou* leave in thirty minutes. I'll take a bath till then."

Farhan nodded. "Aye aye captain."

Hira wondered if her husband had forgotten what had happened, for he seemed so care-free and just by recalling the *shaadi* lights of that day, Hira was now afraid to bathe without leaving the door open.

* * *

Roads away, a car whizzed down the bumpy Phase 6 Street. With his head dangling on the armrest, Mohsin snored to the beats of Alamgir's classics. His brother, who wasn't allowed to switch the station, rushed the car to-wards Gulberg, mainly because his elder sibling's playlist was nauseating.

"With this speed, you'll probably miss a turn and we'll end up in Pindi," Mohsin uttered with his eyes closed. "I wish though – *ghar hi ja phonchain hum.*"

Zaryab shook his head in dismay. "We're going for good home-cooked food to meet three good friends and the least you can do is *pretend* that you're fine."

But Mohsin wasn't fine and he didn't want to put up an act. He had wished to sleep, but had instead travelled with a heavy head, imagining Majhbeen's phupho's face. Now that he thought of it, it seemed like a far-fetched story his *chokidar* would fondly tell him; a story made up with fragments of the truth. But this was a story he had lived through and just thinking about it exhausted him.

"I wanted to ask something or more like say something…" Mohsin said, adjusting himself on the seat.

"If it's about *that* day, I don't want to hear it," came a reply.

"It's not. But it's just a random thought about

Majhbeen's phupho, you know..."

"I mean," Mohsin continued. "Her *bachpan ka* fiancé who fell in love and married someone else and then later died on the wedding night was just a coincidence. Majhbeen showed his photos. He was an addict. Then, two *mangnian* being canceled – it's no such big deal. I mean, our very own sister just woke up one day and canceled her engagement. We still don't know the reason. Then, phupho's first husband disappearing after the wedding night is well – fine, a strange thing. But I feel that it might be because some people are born with bad luck… bad things happen to them, *haina* and *phir* on that eid.."

"I said I don't want to recall that day," Zaryab cut in.

Mohsin's voice trailed off. "Stop the car!"

"What?"

"Damn it, *rouk gaari!*"

Zaryab stomped his foot on the breaks and the car slid sideways. As it did, in slow motion, Mohsin saw a levitating woman inches above the ground, with her face fully covered with a floral *dupatta* - as if she were faceless to begin with – waving at him.

Chapter
3

The Dinner

Quite often in life, we get dragged into uncomfortable situations. In Hira's life, prior to this dinner, which was very upsetting to arrange, there had been a disturbing event. Years ago, when she had been a student in Kinnaird, she and Majhbeen, along with a whole other group, had gone to get matching outfits stitched for the annual Charity Day. They'd go in free slots between afternoon classes and Hira's loud, debating skills came in handy for she ended up getting discounts for them all. Majhbeen started this joke of how the head tailor had fallen in love with Hira. At first, Hira had laughed, amused and enjoying the attention but then, *everyone* started saying, 'Hira *sahiba, kitna naap?'* and though it irked her, she thought that eventually it would stop being funny. However, when Hira had gone to pick up the clothes, Majhbeen had chuckled and had said the same phrase, in front of the other tailors including the master tailor, and he had blushed, and slid his number between the stitched clothes. Hira had been the angriest at that time and yet, without a say, she had guffawed the day away. But now that Majhbeen was to be seated on her dining table, and now that she had been forbidden by Farhan to talk about *what had happened,* all the old incidents that had made her furious at Majhbeen had come back.

"Is the table set, jaan?"

Hira adjusted the floral green mats that she had gotten from Alfatah at a discount. There was one missing, but she had decided that there was no way she'd display her new table mats for old, unwanted guests.

"Yes," Hira replied. "I'll serve juice first and then um, we can all be seated here."

"Baad main larki kehwa bna dain gi?"

Hira rolled her eyes. "Haan, Farhan."

The couple's conversation was interrupted by the doorbell.

"It must be the mutton, I'll get it."

Hira's heart skipped a beat. She had already fetched the mutton ten minutes ago and she knew that one of the guests had arrived. A part of her had wanted all three to come at once so that she could get everything over with.

A minute later, Farhan walked back to the lounge-turned-dining-room, followed by Zaryab and Mohsin. Hira had imagined them to look the same, because that is how their photos on Facebook appeared to be, with captions of living the good life. Well, the good life had worn them out a little. Zaryab had gained a few pounds and his lean body now housed a *tiddi,* and Mohsin looked way out of shape; almost like he had seen a ghost.

"Salam," Hira said, with a smile plastered on her face. "You – you guys look-"

"Awful, I know," Zaryab completed the sentence.

"Oh no, that's not what Hira meant," Farhan cut in.

"I'm glad she noticed, *tu nay tou wou bhi nae kia*. We- um, met with an accident on our way here and I guess Mohsin hadn't slept well, so it hit him a little harder." Zaryab answered.

As the juice was served, the brothers explained what had happened – not what Mohsin had seen, but just the car sliding off part which was blamed on a cat being in the middle of the road.

"These damn stray cats and dogs. They'll be the death of us!" Farhan said.

The four of them sat, with silences in between, catching up on things they had missed in the past years. Zaryab discussed how his parents were making him say *haan* to a model cousin, but he had always been inclined towards *hijabi* girls, and everyone laughed at how hypocritical he was for having dated half the batch. Mohsin was remarkably quiet, and the only thing he did for a good half-hour was gulp down juice. Hira and Farhan shared their stories of the new apartment. And everyone had something to say so that what they *really* had on their minds could not be said.

"Is Majho coming?" Mohsin inquired, requesting another glass of juice.

"I hope she is." Hira replied. "And we're out of juice. Save your appetite for some good ol' mutton."

* * *

2015

The thing about *shaadi* houses is that they stand out. It's not the excessive decor, or the drum *walay*, or the parade of familiar faces, but the fact that the house is either welcoming someone or letting someone go and in both cases, it stands tall, with open gates, all dressed up for the occasion. Majhbeen's house had dolled up many times for her phupho and this time, the lights shone the brightest. They were giving their all, and the house was crowding in on itself with everyone. The tiniest corners had expanded to let everyone in. Something about the whole occasion told Majhbeen that this would be it, phupho's Happily Ever After.

Hira walked inside and sat on the sofa. Her previous place had been taken by an aunty who refused to move and looking at aunty jee's *laddo* size Hira knew she'd not be moving at all.

"Where are the guys?" Majhbeen asked, elbowing her friend. "The baraat is about to arrive."

"Zaryab and Mohsin are on their way and Farhan is standing outside with uncle jee. When will the food be served?"

"Motu, let the baraat *tou* arrive. I have some Slanty *kay* packs resting on the bed upstairs. Go have those."

"Red *walay?*"

Majhbeen nodded.

Smiling, Hira, amidst running children, scampered upstairs. Her hand brushed against the wooden handrail and her khussa squeaked on the marble floor. Paper flowers hung from the fans and frames. Her stomach growled seeing three unopened packets of crisps. She then jumped on one of the pillows, burst open the packets and started gulping down the chips. Lying on the bed had made her realize how tired she had gotten from running around all day. The soles of her feet hurt and all the munching made her want to sleep.

"Perhaps just for a few minutes," she said to herself.

As she placed both her legs on the bed, an unseen thing - or force pushed her legs back to the ground.

Alarmed, Hira stood up and examined her whereabouts. There was no one on the bed or under it. However, the glass window in Majho's room, which gave the view to a large, old tree right in front of where she stood, made her freeze.

On the tree which was wrapped in blinking fairy lights, sat Majhbeen's phupho with her legs sideways like that of a frog. She clung to one of the branches and she wore no clothes. Her sagging breasts and chocolate brown nipples were the first things Hira saw. The second thing Hira noticed was her face; devoid of all innocence, and tongue slithering out of her mouth like a snake. The worst part however was that phupho *jaan* was staring right at Hira, with wide-open, washed-down mascara eyes. In such cases, people run, but Hira stood still, unable to do anything. She had spent nights in that room before and she knew that there was no way phupho could have climbed that tree, and she also knew that the window was merely a soundproof glass design to let the person glimpse outside and served no purpose, especially not that of a window. Nothing from the outside could be heard, and yet the very next moment, Hira heard a hiss. Phupho's tongue went back and forth and the horrid sound of it had been just inches away from Hira's ear. She thought that she would pass out, or scream, but like the tenacious ice stuck to the bottom of a freezer, unable to be scraped off, Hira blankly stood there, drowning in fear.

Chapter

4

Foolish Beliefs

2015

Drenched in sweat, Hira waited for it, whatever it was, to pass like a bad dream. She closed her eyes and remembered her mother, the first time Farhan had held her hand, and the aftertaste of Slanty. Her body had turned on her and the only option left was to wait it out, which is what she did. As she opened her eyes, she saw that the naked creature was gone and that only the view of the tree remained. Quickly, without wearing her *khussay* or grabbing her *chunri dupatta,* Hira sprinted downstairs.

Sitting in the corner, fixing the pearls in her phupho's hair, Majhbeen saw her friend running across the hall, out of breath. Worried, she followed.

"W-what happened?" Majhbeen called out from behind. "Where are you going?"

Hira continued to run, until she spotted Farhan and then instantly broke into tears.

"Are you alright?" Farhan gasped, looking at the makeup, sweat and mucus dripping off Hira's face. *"Huwa kya hai tumhe?"*

"Btao bhi?"

But the only thing that came out of Hira's mouth were hiccups.

Till then, everyone had started to gather around the hysterically sobbing Hira and seeing that, Majhbeen and Farhan, dragged her to the tent being set nearby.

"Would you please tell us what happened?"

"What happened to her?" Farhan repeated.

"I don't know," Majhbeen replied. "She went upstairs to have chips and then she just ran to you!"

The stage was being set but except a few men and waiters, no guest was present in the tent. Hira's sobs had turned into little cries with an occasional 'mama jee, mama jee' between them. A waiter passing by handed over a glass bottle of Coke to Hira.

"Thank you," Farhan replied. "Drink this, Hira. And then tell us what happened."

However, no matter how hard they tried to get it out of her, she wouldn't say anything. The Coke sips gradually stopped the cries, but Hira had this awful feeling that if she spoke, that horrid phupho look-alike would come after her. She had heard of a story from a friend of a friend, whose father had been an exorcist and the story had stayed with her for a long time: 'A molvi once tried to exorcise a young man. He had spiritually healed many and he thought that the man was no exception but the man had no ordinary jinn inside him. It was the devil himself. And it refused to go. One night, the molvi's son saw the man outside their door and not knowing what the man housed in himself, the boy offered him sweets. Then the son saw that the man's feet were twisted. Seeing that, he closed the door and fled inside. But when he entered his room, he saw the same man sitting on his sofa with his back towards him. Not knowing how he could have entered and magically appeared inside, the boy backed away. Then, the man's head started to turn. It turned back like an owl's whilst his body stayed still. The molvi's son fainted. Every time he tried to tell his father what had happened, he saw the jinn-man behind his father.' Somehow, Hira believed that if she stayed quiet, everything would be alright.

"Did someone touch you?" Farhan asked. "Did something bad happen?"

"No one was upstairs, Farhan," Majhbeen replied.

"Let her talk. Did someone say something or *do* something?"

Hira shook her head. "No," she said.

Before Farhan and Majhbeen could persuade Hira any further, the waiter informed them that the baraat had arrived.

"Do you want me to wait here with you?" Farhan asked. "Majhbeen can go, I can wait."

"It's alright," Hira replied. "Let's just all go."

Hira was barefoot and so Majhbeen ran upstairs to fetch her things and after powdering her face, led her back inside. The brothers too had arrived, and the festive rituals started. The women had prepared some dances, and the men competed with them, which was followed by the food being served. During all this, Hira couldn't help but notice how well-kept and happy phupho was, seated on the stage with not a care in the world. Deep down, she felt sick. It was not the kind of sickness you feel whirling round and round on Murree's roads, but the kind you get when you know something awful is going to happen. Majhbeen's house was now empty and everyone was present in the tent for the *rukhsati*. Hira overheard uncle that no Quran could be found in the house to place over the bride's head. One by one, the family members went inside to fetch their own Quran or *suparay* from the lounge, but each returned empty-handed. They decided to proceed without it, and Hira made sure that she sat as far away from phupho as possible.

The lights went dim and the crowd gathered around the newlyweds to bid them a blessed life ahead. Hira wasn't the only one who didn't feel right. Mohsin, who had been busy video calling a Brazilian friend, noticed how the rose petals instead of falling on the bride, were mysteriously blown away to the side. There was no wind, and yet no flower landed on the phupho. He shrugged the feeling off and asked Zaryab if they could leave.

"Bus end *ho raha hai,* we'll leave with the group in fifteen. *Ja kar* Gloria *bethtey hain."*

Sometimes in life, things are sudden, rapid and continuous. You know, when uncle dies, then chacha falls sick, then bhai loses his job, and that cavity you thought needed filling turns out to be needing a root canal. And just like that, with what Hira had seen and felt, the lights in the tent went off. It was pitch dark, and only the torches of the phone shone on strangers' faces. Before anyone could tell the event planner to turn the lights back on, a shrieking scream was heard. Not a human's or perhaps a human's who was in extreme agony, followed by the sound a cat makes when someone steps on its tail.

When Hira had gotten married, she had made sure that the door-bell would be of her choice. She had spent ages trying to convince her ami to have a simple tuned bell, but her ami had always adored 'happy birthday to you' and 'merry Christmas and a happy new year' tones and every time it had rung, she had been embarrassed.

Those twenty years of shame had led her to find the perfect simple tune for her not so perfect apartment.

Ding dong.

"That must be Majhbeen." Farhan said. "Please excuse me."

Farhan had always had the greatest time with the boys. Especially without the girls, to whom they easily handed all the projects to, the days were priceless. Drives, country-wide adventures, and *karrak* road-side *chai* over talks they couldn't otherwise have. However, today he had run out of things to say and now that the bell had rung, he had the perfect excuse to leave the room.

"It's raining." Hira said. "Hurry. *Geeli na hou jaye wou.*"

The gate opened to a slightly soaked Majhbeen who hurriedly handed a box of Cakes and Bakes to Farhan.

"Hello Majho."

"Hey…Farhan, would you be having a change of five-hundred rupees or maybe two-forty..I came on Uber."

"Oh *haan, haan.* Wait, let me get my wallet."

"Sahab!" a man yelled and Farhan looked up; it was the driver, waving from the car.

"Nae chahiyen koyi bhi paisay! Allah hafiz!" Saying that frantically, he steered the car off the street. His Bismillah chants could be heard until he reached the society's gate.

"Geez, what happened to him? Never seen an Uber driver not want cash."

"I- I don't know."

"It's alright, come in."

Farhan closed the door behind him, not knowing the horror that awaited him.

Chapter
5

It's Not An Indian Drama

From the corner of the room, the table could be seen. Old china had been used, and there was a seat for the sixth person for whom the dishes had not been laid out, but the food smelled delicious. Farhan had kept everyone's choice in mind; Majhbeen who ate the Main Canteen's sad Chinese back in university (Sweet and Sour by chacha Khan made with *biryani masala),* Mohsin who was very fond of mutton chops, and Lasagna for himself and the *begum.* He was not sure what Zaryab liked, but he believed that the diverse feast would be enjoyable.

"Let's begin," Farhan said.

"Won't we say our prayer first, father?" Zaryab joked and everyone forced a laugh.

"Let *bhabhi* come," Mohsin replied.

"Oh, I'll help get her from the kitchen," Majhbeen said, nervously licking the lipstick on her lips.

"No, no… you start. *Wou ati hou gi,* she went to get

the ice-cubes." Farhan insisted. *"Chalo sab, shabash."*

A time which previously was spent in food fights, and mimicry, and funny remarks was now being spent in silence.

"Kitchen *hai kahan?*" Majhbeen asked. "I'll go get Hira. I need to use the washroom anyway."

Maybe if it had been you and I, we would have accompanied our guest, but Farhan was too hungry to move and with the spinach lasagna strips churning between his teeth, he thought not to. Plus, in his defense, it was an apartment with two rooms; how hard could it be for the guest to find his wife?

"The kitchen is on the left. It was actually the living-room but we broke it and made it into the kitchen and um- both the rooms are open. Use any washroom you please."

Majhbeen smiled and excused herself.

Everyone knew that from the lot, Majhbeen was the least well-off, not that it had ever mattered, and with her scholarship suspended during the last term, the boys had come together and paid for the semester. There were days when they all ate KFC, whereas Majhbeen chose to stay back for the desi Chinese and Hira being the friend she had been, always brought a Kentucky for her if Majho refused to tag along. However, amidst that, Majhbeen had always been chirpy, well dressed, and organized. She usually covered the tip of her nose in red tint in an attempt to look cute, and it worked. Things change in hours and five years is in fact a long, long time. However, the Majhbeen that they had now seen, worried them. Her clothes were shabby, so much so that the color had been drained out of them. Her hair looked like a bird's nest. She fumbled here and there in a clueless manner and she didn't smell of sweat but instead of a dead man and rotten *sabzi.*

"We should ask her."

"What?"

"We should ask her guys," Mohsin suggested, after Majhbeen left the table. "If she needs help or not."

"I don't think she'll appreciate that," Farhan answered. "I mean she's married."

"Haan *tou?*"

"Bura na lag jaye."

"I agree with Farhan," Zaryab interjected. "We can maybe go collectively to her place with gifts *wagera* but we don't even know how she'll take that."

"Come on, *yaar.* Majho *hai.* She'll know where it's coming from. We care, that's it. She looks really upset."

"Hmm."

"Acha the mutton is great. Did Hira make it?"

"Nae Z. But don't tell her I told you, just appreciate my *biwi."*

The three laughed and this time, it had been genuine.

Mohsin was seated with his back towards the door, where the head of the family sits- but of course, there were no such rules in Farhan's house. The seat opposite to him was empty, and nestled on both his sides were the guys, next to whom the girls sat. As he devoured the chops, he saw a little boy walk in, and sit on the seat across from him. He was a happy little lad- perhaps ten years of age, with a huge smile on his face. Farhan seemed to ignore his existence and Mohsin assumed him to be the house-help similar to the *chotu* he had on the construction site.

The boy started to eat from Farhan's plate, placing chunks of meat in his mouth with some falling from between his fingers but Farhan didn't seem to mind the least. Mohsin shrugged.

His attention was diverted by Hira walking in with a tray full of drinks.

"I didn't want to serve you guys juice again so I fixed us some margaritas. Am I not the best?"

"Begum is the best."

"Thanks, *bhabhi,*" Zaryab replied. "Majho *nae ayi?*"

"Hain?"

"She went to the kitchen to assist you." Farhan replied. "Maybe she's in the washroom. Could you go check? I'll warm her plate."

"Oh, *mera pass tou nae ayi…*" Hira answered, walking out. She signaled Farhan to not have any more lasagna (you know, Lahori women and their priorities).

As Hira left the room, Mohsin saw the small boy following her. If it was possible, Mohsin thought that the boy had gotten remarkably bigger from when he had walked in.

"Since when do you have house help?" Moshin asked, letting his curiosity get the best of him. "Our *chotu* can only serve *chai.* But I really like how you treat him like one of your own."

"Hain Farhan?" he continued.

"Oh, I thought you were talking to Zaryab. I don't understand."

"Oho, *bacha kab say ghar kaam kar raha hai.* It's not like I'll tell on you for child labour, haha."

Puzzled, Farhan placed the lasagna on the far end of the table. "We don't have any house help. At least not yet. Hira *keh keh kar thak gae hai* but honestly whoever comes, isn't up to her standards. *Ab* just yesterday *hi,* an elderly woman came who made such delicious *chappatis* but Hira said that she was too slow. What can a man do?"

"Mama jee is always looking for *din raat ki* maids too," Zaryab said. "Apparently, a good one is very hard to find."

"*Tou* who was the *chota bacha,* that child who came and ate from your plate?" Mohsin inquired.

"Which plate and when?"

"Oh *yaar*, just now a boy came, sat…" Mohsin pointed towards the chair across from him, "…there and he ate from your plate and you didn't say anything."

Farhan looked at Zaryab who himself appeared to have no clue about what his brother was on about. Before coming, his brother had seen a face-less woman in thin air, which had almost cost them their lives. They had been lucky that there had been no car in sight, and now he kept insisting that a boy had entered the room and eaten food. But before he could calm his brother down, Hira walked in.

"Did Majhbeen leave?" Hira asked, confused. "Because she's nowhere in the house. *Chapa chapa chan mara hai.*"

"How could she leave?" Hira inquired, annoyed.

"Of course, she didn't leave yaar. Her bag is still here and look, so is her phone."

Beside an untouched plate of food lay a shut-off phone and an presumably empty clutch.

"Good, now I can't even call her and ask why she left!" Hira scoffed.

"She hasn't left." Farhan replied, getting up. "If you guys don't mind, I'll go look for her. Hira can't find things in front of her so I don't expect her to find Majhbeen."

"Yeah right." Hira replied, rolling her eyes.

"We'll join you guys." Zaryab replied. "I'm almost done."

"What if she heard us offering help, got embarrassed and left?" Farhan said. "God!"

"What did you guys say?"

"Oh *nae bhai*. She wasn't there and nothing we said was offensive." Zaryab answered. "You said she came on an uber *tou* she couldn't have ordered one without her phone."

"And she didn't have any money." Farhan added. "She previously asked me for some."

"Drinks *bnane kya gae, duniya idhar say udher ho gae!*" Hira exclaimed, with irritation in her voice.

"Guys, guys stop. We'll all go look for her. Even if she did leave, she wouldn't have gotten very far. *But,* before we go, I need to declutter my mind. Who the hell was that boy who ate from Farhan's plate?" Mohsin inquired. "And I'm asking seriously."

"I have no idea what you guys are on about. I'll fetch my bag, Farhan and *bhaion* then let's go."

"For the last time Mohsin, we don't have any house help, only Hira and I live in this house. There's no little boy. The joke isn't funny anymore, *yar.* And I ate food from my plate." Farhan answered.

"But…"

"*Chal bhai,*" Zaryab said. "We can discuss it later."

But Mohsin didn't want to discuss it later. He followed the others outside, and as he did, he noticed roti crumbs under the sixth seat.

Chapter
6

Where is Majhbeen?

When Majhbeen had been young, she had wandered off to the park alone. Her ami wasn't the awfully careful kind. She had *syaape* of her own to deal with; problems that well, could not just be called problems. Her daughter was her phupho's responsibility, who was a great caretaker. Phupho had gone to boil milk and *shakar* for little Majho, something Majho really liked, and during that time Majho had escaped from the backdoor to the nearby park. It wasn't her fault or phupho's. Back in the village, everyone roamed everywhere and returned home before the sunset. Frantic that someone in the city had kidnapped Majho, phupho had started weeping and Majho's ami had sat on the sofa and sipped the *shakar doodh*. An hour later, the neighbor's son had knocked on phupho's door with Majhbeen clinging to his hand.

"She was sitting by herself in the park. They were going to close it. I asked her where she lived-"

Phupho had hugged Majhbeen and with tears rolling down her cheeks, had scolded herself for leaving the child unattended.

"I had a splendid time!" the child had told phupho. "I had seen a tree in which fairies appeared. They hung upside down and continuously whispered. They were angry when the uncle took me back home."

Phupho had laughed with amusement.

* * *

2015

The *shaadi* tent was quiet except for a few mumbling sounds. The background titanic tuned music had stopped. No one knew who had screamed, and there was no way to find out because everything was pitch dark.

"F-F-Farhan…" Hira whispered. "What the hell was that?"

"Probably some aunty who got scared of the load shedding."

"Didn't sound like an aunty." Hira gulped. The only thing she desperately wanted was to go home, wash the scent of slanty off her fingers and then sleep on her ami's bed.

A few men were heard scolding the event planner outside, and within the minutes following it, the light came back on; fluttering bulbs turning on one by one from the back to the front.

"Phew."

"They deliberately turned off the light so that we'd empty the tent. Government *kay* orders *hain,* no?"

"*Nae,* they usually dim the lights, not blankly shut them off." Farhan answered.

People had just had time to collect themselves, when

someone from the front row, probably the video maker since he had a camera in his hand, pointed out that the groom was under the stage.

"Why's he under the stage?" someone asked.

"No, that's just a shadow."

"Where is the *dulha?*"

As the men moved forward, the groom was indeed found under the stage.

"Is everything alright?" he was asked. But the *dulha* was quiet. "He's not feeling well. Quick, someone bring some *thanda* soda!"

Hira, Mohsin, Zaryab, and Farhan made their way toward the entrance. "The *dulha* wants to spend time with the *dulhan*. It's everyone's cue to leave!" Zaryab joked. "Let's just hand the money to phupho and leave."

The poor groom who had just been taken out from under the stage was shivering to the extent that he could not hold the glass. His mother was holding him together and his father, the oldest man Hira had ever seen, was forcing the diet pepsi down his son's throat.

"Majhbeen," Hira said, moving forward. "We're going to leave *yar*. We've wished phupho."

"Stay a while longer. Everyone is leaving Hiroo."

"Haan *tou* we should too *na*. I'll call you in the morning?"

"Please stay. *Bus* ten minutes *tak nikal jana.*"

"Hmm. Let me ask the guys."

Mohsin was on the stage, handing an envelope to phupho who kept refusing. Her hands were hidden somewhere in her *dupatta* so he didn't know what to do. He tried placing it in her lap but she fiddled and told him to take it back. Confused, Mohsin signaled Majhbeen. This wasn't his first time handing over *salami,* and he knew this much that after some tries no one refuses to keep the money.

"Hand them over to Sheryar *bhai.*" Majhbeen instructed. "Phupho *nahin lain gi.*"

By then, most of the tent had been emptied. The first ones to leave had been the food hoarders, followed by aunties who had run out of gossip and couples whose toddlers had vomited food on the carpet. Now, a few outsiders, the guys, Hira and the immediate family remained.

Reluctantly, Mohsin moved towards the groom, not because he was hesitant to hand over the three thousand rupees tucked in a pink envelope, but because as a child, when things wouldn't feel right, he would get very anxious, short of breath if you must say. And the denseness of the air grew as he approached Sheryar bhai.

"Salam," he said. "I hope you're feeling better now."

The groom looked at him and nodded.

"We are Majhbeen's friends. She's like a sister to us. This is something from us."

Saying that, he held the envelope in front of the groom. Sheryar bhai calmly placed his hand first on the envelope, a loose grip that made Mohsin hold on for a little longer, and then bhai jaan moved his fingers on top of Mohsin's bony hand and firmly held it.

Mohsin smiled. *"Yeh apke liye."*

The groom pressed his hand tighter.

"Haha, haath choriye."

At this point, Mohsin tried not only to pull back, but to snatch away the envelope, so that his hand could break free. The groom grinned sheepishly, with his face fixed in one place and his little almond shaped pupils eyeing Mohsin.

"Haath chorain..mera."

"Sheryar, *beta, haath choro bache ka.*" A woman standing behind the groom commanded.

Mohsin had arm-wrestled all his life, and put on those gigantic Nestle bottles on the dispenser which was a sign of manly power for a then nineteen-year-old, but Sheryar bhai's grasp felt like that of a machine's and the more Mohsin tried to slide away his fingers, the more bhai's palm locked into his. Before Mohsin could call out for help, Sheryar sahab opened his hand, and his dilated eyes returned back to normal, revealing emotions.

"The hell, man!" Mohsin said. "Are you out of your mind?"

"Jee?" the groom asked, stunned, oblivious to what he had just done, as if he had simply zoned out.

"You were trying to fracture my hand with all that twisting!"

The groom opened his mouth to answer, and his tongue came out followed by foam- white and yellow, a scene of a washing machine exploding, and after a few jerks, he fell on Mohsin's shoes and lost consciousness.

* * *

The drizzle had turned into heavy rain, befriended by a howling breeze and the rough rustling of the leaves whose sound rudely knocked the doors of Lahore. The four had searched what the elders would say *chapa chapa* of the house and Majhbeen hadn't been found. The main gate had been locked from the inside which meant that she possibly couldn't be outside, but they had still left, armed with umbrellas in the brother's car to look for her. The streets on the sides ahead within the colony were too narrow for the vehicle to drive through, and so they had stepped out, calling out her name.

This continued for a good half hour, till they gave up and returned back home.

"It may sound selfish but *khuda ki kasam*, I haven't had anything since *subah* and I need to eat." Hira moaned. "If I eat, maybe I can look for her better."

"Ghar hi ja rahe hain. Thoos lena." Farhan replied. "But guys, we seriously need to call her home or something. Phone *bhi yahan,* bag *bhi* and *lapata bhi."*

"Drive me home and you can look for her all you want." Mohsin said. "Honestly, I don't give a damn."

"Ouch?"

"Don't be offended, bro. I'm really thankful for the dinner, dil say. But everything about today is reminding me of the old bullshit and I'm just not up for it."

"Bhai…" Farhan replied. *"…ehsan nae kia aa kar.* And nothing is wrong with anything or anyone. You're out of your mind. Seeing boys and shit. And then instead of helping ease a legitimate worry, you want to go home?"

"Acha Farhan *tu tou thanda ho."* Zaryab interrupted. "We're grownups now. Let us go home. I assure you we won't leave unless Majhbeen is found. You have my word."

The drive back was silent, except for Hira's pesky humming which no one said anything about. Mohsin, with his arms crossed, sat with his head out the window. As the cold wind parted his hair, he felt at ease. 'Maybe I just need a good night's sleep,' he said to himself. 'There's nothing a good night's sleep can't solve.'

Seated in the lounge, with Hira and Zaryab gobbling down food, Mohsin and Farhan patiently waited for Majhbeen's phone to charge.

"This is our only option." Farhan said. "What if it has a passcode or something?"

"Tou phir we'll have to think of something else." Mohsin answered. "Is the charger working? I don't see any light."

"I don't know. Hira *kay purane phone ka hai.* Hira,

could you come and check?"

Hira hopped down from the sofa and examined the phone. "I can't believe she hasn't changed her phone in five years."

"And yes, *abhi on hou jata hai.*"

"If it turns on, I'm going to call any number from her recent calls and tell them what happened."

"Let Hira call." Farhan said. "Husband mind *na kar jaye.* Also don't tell them what happened. Just ask about Majho."

The conversation shifted briefly to the new LED screens with built-in android and then when the phone's beep was heard, the group stopped talking. Hira ran towards the phone.

"Okay….okay…"

"It's on! No passcode!"

"Great." Farhan said. "Now call the last dialed number."

Hira zoomed into the wallpaper which was of Majhbeen and a man, probably her husband. "Guys, Majho's husband is so old. He looks like he's forty or something."

"Dekhana?"

"Baad main dekhna yaar, Mohsin." Zaryab replied. "Hira, just call and ask."

"Oh, alright. The last call is to 'Rashid ami'. I'm assuming it is Majhbeen's mother-in-law. Should I call? I mean what if she doesn't know that Majhbeen came to meet us. Won't we get her into trouble?"

"Good point. *Aur* who has he called?"

"There's an incoming call from 'massi 2' at 6p.m. Probably the house-help. *Mila doun?*"

"Haan" the brothers said at once.

Hira sandwiched herself between Zaryab and Farhan

and called the number. An old classic song played for a second and then a woman picked up from the other end.

"Hello?"

"Salam!" Hira said, turning on the loudspeaker. *"Main Majhbeen baji ki saheli baat kar rahi houn. Baat ho sakti hai?"*

"Jee aik minute. Wou upper kamre main hain."

"I knew she bloody went home." Hira said furiously. "So rude."

Following the sound of thumping footsteps, the phone reached upstairs.

"Hello?"

"Hey, it's me Hira."

"Of course I know it's you, Hiroo. I was just about to call you. I'm so sorry that I couldn't come today. Actually, Rashid came back today morning which was unexpected so the whole family is in Pindi *warna* I *tou* had informed my *saas* beforehand…"

Chapter
7

We're Being Tricked

When Mohsin was seven and growing up –when he could no longer bathe with his baby sister in a pool, he realized that he could see things. Things that other people could not see. Things that did not reveal themselves to others. Horrible, horrible things. Once, as he recalls, the whole family was outside some *masjid* in Islamabad. His cousin who was about to get married had booked the whole mosque for his *nikkah* and had bragged about it for the longest time. However, Mohsin saw two weddings happen that day. He saw that on the farthest corner of the masjid, where some unused speakers were kept, there was a herd of odd-looking people. They were shiny blue, with hollow sockets, and long chins. Some of them had their tongues out. He distinctly remembered that because when he returned back home, he tried to stretch his tongue and make it droop down till his Adam's apple which of course had just resulted in a headache. These people, they didn't enter through the door. They came through the walls, and each time Mohsin rubbed his eyes to snap out of the dream, more people appeared. One of those blue people, a little boy-girl (Mohsin could not decipher what species it was, let alone what gender) came up to him. Amused, and he did not know for what reason (probably because he was a child) he tried to take the *barfi* type *mithae* out of its hand. Not only did it look delicious, but he couldn't help notice how different its fragrance was. So he decided to take it, because he didn't know any better, and when he did, the girl-boy bent down and bit him on his leg. Moshin screamed in agony. He could feel crooked nails piercing through his *shalwar* and diving deep into this flesh. But when his ami checked what had happened, the skin wasn't the slightest bit hurt.

"Stop being so dramatic." he had been told. "One day you'll be getting married. Do you want your cousin Akbar to ruin your wedding by screaming like that?"

* * *

2015

The people gathered around the stage and carried the *dulha* to one of the sofas in the first row. Mohsin was stunned and so, he politely excused himself from the scene. At this point, phupho jaan had started sobbing. Majhbeen had rushed to console her and other aunties could be heard saying 'Not this time. Nothing will happen. Sheryar has had nothing to eat. *Aisay ho jata hai.'* The crowd lessened and gradually the people left till only Majhbeen's *abu,* his hairy mustached friend, Sheryar bhai's *ami,* and the group remained.

"We should leave." Moshin said, elbowing his brother. "The function is over. What else is there to do?"

"It's been a long day. The stupid waiter spilled coke on my waistcoat. Let's miss Gloria *wala plan* and head home." Zaryab replied.

The two shook hands with Farhan, smiled at Majhbeen, handed over snacks from their vehicle's trunk to Hira, and started the jeep.

"Do you think the *dulha* will be alright?" Mohsin asked. "I mean, he looked pretty pale."

"I don't know. Poor phupho. I hope she's alright."

"Let me put on Nusrat. I can't listen to your songs," Mohsin continued.

"No."

"Acha aik mera, aik apka."

"Highway *per* I'll listen to my jam."

"Fine." Mohsin agreed. "Play Nusrat *filhaal.*"

Zaryab had just reversed the vehicle when he spotted Majhbeen's father coming outside.

He waved at the boys, who waved back, thinking it was a goodbye, but then he knocked at the window. He signaled them to stop. "Are you in a hurry?"

"Bus uncle," Zaryab said, lowering the window. *"Ama akeli hain.* We thought we should leave now. Plus *kal subah class hui."*

"I have a favor to ask, if it is not too much." uncle requested. "Only if it isn't too much."

"Of course, uncle."

"Wou, Sheryar isn't in a state to drive and my car isn't in a state to be driven for a *dulha,* you know, *bhenoyi* protocol and all. I have to drop Bashir, my friend. Majhbeen can accompany you if you can drop her phupho and Sheryar. *Yeh pass hi,* Canal View housing society main. *Raaste main hi hai, beta."*

"Uncle don't worry. *Raaste main na bhi hota tou* we would have dropped them. Please send them."

The workers had started dissembling the tent, so Farhan and Hira too stood outside, waiting for Farhan to finish his smoke. The plan later changed to Zaryab and Mohsin dropping the groom and his mother, and Majhbeen and the bride sitting in Farhan's car for she needed to fetch her medicines.

"Sheryar said that we'd get them on our way home. A new asthma kit, so I didn't send my old one with the *samaan.* I didn't know he'd get unwell…"

"Phupho jaan," Hira cut in. "You don't have to explain. Pick up a new one from the pharmacy if you want. We'll drop you to Canal View after that."

And so the two cars, Farhan's extensively-used City and the brother's 1998 Pajero, set on the road. The decorated stationary Suzuki with now wilted flowers and partially brown taped leaves could be seen from the rearview mirror.

* * *

Quite often in life, you lose a thing and when you *really* can't find it, you start to think about *massi* Kalsoom's intentions or the fact that your little *bhai* must have broken it because you're so sure of where you had kept it. But what happens if you *lose a person* or if the missing person isn't lost in the first place?

"I don't understand any of this!" Hira exclaimed.

The four of them sat in a circle, which they hadn't made deliberately, trying to tell each other that there was a possible explanation for what had happened.

"She came on a video call and sent us her location. She really is cities away. So who was that person that we let into our house and fed?"

"Stop talking about it." Farhan replied to his wife.

"There's no use. It makes no sense. The more we talk about it, the more troubled we'll get."

"What if-"

"Yaar, Mohsin.."

"Nae, listen," Mohsin replied. "What if it *really was* Majhbeen?"

"What?"

"Five years ago at her phupho's wedding, you know how Sheryar bhai acted when I was handing him the envelope, mumbling, ghostly, *pata nae*. And the moment he snapped back to his senses, he didn't remember anything. What if Majhbeen came and she doesn't remember?"

"Right, right, right…" Hira mocked. "What about her husband who I said salam to? Would he not have reported a missing wife? And last I knew Majho couldn't fly because that's the only way she could have gotten to Pindi."

Mohsin knew that there was an unnatural explanation to it; he firmly believed so. His heart was sinking and his breath collecting into little icy *golay*, which was to say that something wasn't right. But then again, his body was also telling him that he badly needed sleep.

"I…um… Zaryab, is it fine if we stay the night?"

"You definitely should. How impolite of us to not have asked. It's no use driving back now. And there's a separate-"

"I don't think so." Zaryab replied, looking at Hira. "You've been very hospitable. It'll be too much. We can crash in PC, and then head off after breakfast *kal.*"

"Bhai jee, I know *bohut paisa hai*. Room with breakfast and all but I too make great scrambled eggs and *thora* English *karna hai tou* I can make pancakiaan *too.*"

Farhan laughed. "Don't underestimate my *begum* and

please, I insist. Stay."

Before Zaryab could reply, Mohsin jumped up with all the energy left in him. "Hira, be a darling and take me to the room. I need to put my thoughts to rest."

For quite some time, perhaps since they had shifted in, Hira had always wanted to have guests over. She had known that the place was small, but it wasn't unwelcoming and with her artsy skills, she had turned it into a homely, albeit crowded, apartment. She hadn't expected her first guest to be Mohsin but showing him around made her proud. There were three scented soaps to choose from, and cocomo packets on the scented-candle stand. She wasn't providing less than a five-star experience herself.

"Tell me what you want for breakfast." Hira inquired.

"Whatever you can make." came a reply. "Please turn off the lights on your way out."

Hira nodded and quietly shut the door.

"The wind has stopped and I've given him the coziest bed sheet. Your brother will sleep like a baby." she said, placing herself on a beanbag in the lounge.

The guys spent a good time browsing through the tv-channels, expecting to see a new thing on the third way around. Soon, they gave up and settled on the Avenger's ending.

"Are you two not sleepy?" Hira asked.

"Not me."

"Me neither."

"But if you want to sleep," Farhan replied, "go ahead. I'll join you in a bit."

"I've had too much to eat. I'll make *kehwa* first. If you guys want some, please let me know."

"*Sonf wala?*" Zaryab asked, with a hopeful tone.

"Now you can underestimate the *begum*. She will give you Tapal's sachet in hot water and you'll have to praise how perfectly hot the water is…or how balanced the ratio of water is to..”

"Haha, very funny!" Hira smirked. "So two *kehwas?*"
"Two *kehwas.*"

Hira turned on the stove and sat near it watching the little bubbles appear on the surface. She often wondered at what point the water started to become warm, and then gradually boiling hot. And she was just wondering that when the light above her head flickered. It wasn't the first time the bulb had fused so thinking that she'd tell Farhan to change it in the morning, she let the thought slide. The light continued to flicker, and eventually, Hira got up and turned it off. When she tried turning it back on – the only existing light in the kitchen, because turning something off and on in desi households always helped to fix it, the bulb refused to cooperate. After several tries, when it flashed for a second or so, sitting on the stove with the fire ranging between her thighs, was a grinning Majhbeen with her head tilted to the side, almost dangling off, and her bushy hair stirring the water.

"Kehwa piye gi tu?" came a sound from her, without her lips moving.

* * *

Chapter
8

Majhbeen Didn't Leave the House

Mohsin lay on the guest bed, counting the cracks in the ceiling. When he had gone for his masters abroad, they had enrolled him in an optional psychology course. His artistic side had enjoyed it a lot. In it, a popular way to go to sleep decades back had been to count the number of sheep on a cardboard paper. Moshin lay in bed counting the cracks, pretending they were moving sheep. He thought that at any moment, he would fall into a deep slumber and dream of what men often dream about; happiness. But, he could not forget what had happened that day. He envied his brother for being so easygoing about the occurrence. He didn't care about Farhan or Hira, so their obliviousness and casual behavior didn't bother him. He really wanted Zaryab to understand that he was suffering and that he had been for a long time. He was doing something for a living that he disliked, following his father's wishes, and killing his own. He had not slept well in ages because he saw the creatures from his nightmares at superstores and work sites. And he felt like he was in his ami's kheer dish; she kept stirring it, and he kept swallowing *badam* bits, trying to stay afloat. The misery was never-ending. The Majhbeen mystery was just a cherry on top.

There were twenty-seven abu cracks, twenty medium sized ami cracks and eight baby cracks in Farhan's guest room ceiling and this counting was only till where the lamp's light went. Mohsin was still at it, when he heard a scream from outside. Startled, he got up at once.

"What- what happened?" he asked, opening the door.

The television was on but the guys were not present in the lounge.

"Farhan? Zaryab?"

"In the kitchen!" his brother's voice came and Mohsin followed it.

"What happened?" he asked again.

"We- we don't know," Zaryab replied. "Hira was making *kehwa,* she suddenly yelled and lost consciousness. Farhan just carried her to their room."

"Should we go?"

"Let him come outside. You know how Hira was back in university. She fainted twice in front of us, once on her own birthday surprise, and once when she wasn't allowed to sit for the financial management exam. *Yaad hai na.*"

"*Haan...*" Moshin replied. "But what happened in the kitchen?"

"Cockroach *dekh liya hou ga.*" Zaryab shrugged. "I don't know."

"What I am saying is,' he continued, "that it is no big deal."

After what seemed like the longest minute, Farhan came outside and quietly closed the door behind him.

"She's fine." he said. "Feverish and sleep-talking. I gave her a Relaxin to help her sleep."

"Did you ask her what happened?" Mohsin inquired.

"I did and she said something about Majhbeen's vagina on fire."

"What?"

"Haha, yeah…" Farhan replied. "I guess you're not the only one who needed sleep."

"You both are taking this *very* lightly!" Mohsin exclaimed.

"It's Hira…" Farhan answered. "Drama's her middle name. She'll be fine, trust me."

But Mohsin did not trust Farhan. He did not trust anyone. Knowing that no one was as concerned as him, he stomped back to his room. This time, he didn't need to count the cracks. Sleep came to him.

* * *

2015

Hira's nano often used to say that there was magic in the *ruksati* period. Every daughter needs to have a proper one, to safeguard a happily ever after. The mama, papa, and *khalaein* all walk together to the car and send the couple off to their home. The groom and bride aren't to be separated till they reach the house because if they part, happiness slips through; at least that's what nano believed.

'But this is different.' Hira thought. 'The bride and groom are sitting in different cars, and going the opposite way only to join again.'

Hira slowly started taking the pins out of phupho's hair – there were so many of them, and she wanted them out because phupho's head hurt. Hira had no pins in her hair and her head hurt too. She wanted to tell phupho that she'd seen her naked double, perhaps an evil doppelganger. But most importantly, she wanted to whisper Bismillah in phupho's ear so that she'd know phupho wasn't the devil herself.

'Snap out of it!' Hira told herself. 'Hafiz-e-Quran *hain phupho.* She's anything but a *sheytan.'*

And so, Hira dug her hand deeper into the frizzled curls to get out any remaining bobby pins. Instead of her hand meeting the hard aluminum material, she felt something slimy between her fingers, brushing alongside her nails. She clutched onto it, and pulled it out. There was no light in the car, but that of the lampposts the car passed by, and she held it till they turned around a corner where a billboard's light shone straight into the car. Disgusted, she saw a wiggling caterpillar-like insect swirling itself around the tip of her finger.

Flinching back in fright, she threw the insect towards Majhbeen, and started rubbing her hand with her friend's shirt. "Ew mama jee..ew ew gross..*haye* Allah!"

"What is wrong with you, *peechay ho!*"

"An insect came out of phupho's hair. It was sticking to the scalp!"

"*Tou,* she was on the stage all night, something must have gotten in. I'll take the pins out myself."

"Don't get offended Majhbeen." Hira replied. "She's a phupho to me too, *acha."*

"Okay, okay *larkion!*" phupho intervened. "Don't fight. You can both take out the pins and I'm sorry Hira that an insect came out. No doubt the parlor *wali* made a nest out of my hair."

"Must have been a large pin. Hira and her imagination…" Majhbeen muttered under her breath.

"I know what an insect is." Hira said to herself. "Don't even know why I'm friends with her in the first place.

Weirdo *ki personality samaj hi nahin ati.*"

* * *

2015

Zaryab was a young man of little words, but he *did* understand his brother. Back in that car, driving around in circles, even five years ago, he understood him. He knew what Mohsin wanted, and he deeply cared, but all that he felt for him, was overcome by his father's desires. Knowing that the least he could do was listen to his brother, he handed the aux cord to Mohsin.

"Play your stupid Nusrat." he smiled.

"Beta," a voice came from the backseat, *"ruk jao."*

"But aunty," Zaryab answered, "we're three streets away from the address you gave. This is E block."

"Sheryar doesn't feel well. He wants to get off. You can drop me home."

"What?"

"Ama *ki baat sun lain.* Stop the car."

"Where do you want to go?"

"Home." Sheryar replied. "I want to go home."

"And we *are* going home, Sheryar bhai. Why do you want me to stop midway?"

"If you're feeling unwell, we can speed up the car?" Mohsin added.

"Please just stop the car."

Zaryab pressed the accelerator. "Just six minutes Sheryar-"

"I said stop the car!" The *dulha's* voice sounded hoarse enough to freeze Zaryab's feet. It felt like an order from above and just like that, the car stopped. Without saying anything, Sheryar got out and vanished into the darkness, perhaps the street nearby, if we were to be less dramatic about it. But at that point, from the brothers' and the scared ami's sight, who had never seen his son act out like that, Sheryar disappeared into nothingness.

"He... something is so so wrong!" his mother wept. "They told me not to marry my son to the witch but she stunned him with her *adaein* and *kehkay* and now my son is not my son!"

The brothers remained quiet. They did not know what to say. But deep down, they knew that phupho was anything but a witch. She had taught them how to balance sheets and made them *poori channay* on Sundays.

"We will drop you home." they said.

"Or do you want us to go after Sheryar bhai?" Zaryab inquired. "He wouldn't have gotten far."

"No. I need to go meet my *peer*. You take me home."

Zaryab's body ached. He felt like he was a part of a Bollywood movie; the kind that no one watched. 'That's it!' he told himself. 'Enough of all this.' He then sped his way to Sheryar's house.

"If the groom goes missing, it bloody isn't on me!" he told his brother. "I'm going to drop the lady home and then we're switching off our phones, grabbing coffee, and heading the hell home."

Mohsin nodded.

The car dashed from house to house, till aunty jee pointed at her porch. It took them a few minutes, much less than the estimated five and as Mohsin led aunty inside, he saw Sheryar sitting on the *charpae,* watching them in amusement.

"Main *jeet gya.*"

Chapter
9

Rumors and Broken Friendships

2015

The night of phupho's wedding had been long and tiresome. The five were back in their rooms, each having the weirdest thoughts. Zaryab was seated on his squeaky couch, the one he never let his ami get rid of, and was thinking of never marrying because to him, it seemed nothing less than a burden. He also decided that the very next morning he would talk to his parents about sending him and Mohsin to Australia for the exchange program. Mohsin, who was busy skimming through an old *afsana* he had found on his father's shelf, was feeling sorry for phupho. He believed that this time around, she had been married to a psychopath. Hira, who had generously distributed all her slanty packets to the house-help's daughter, for she felt disgusted by them, still couldn't get the image of naked phupho out of her mind. She planned on telling what she had seen to Mariam, a religious class fellow. Farhan's thoughts weren't actually eerie, unless you count the regret of not being able to ride a 'two tires *wali* cycle' being weird. He wasn't concerned about the past night. Farhan adored Hira, that part was true, but his personality, before marriage at least, was less concerning than it was now. And so, after realizing that there would hardly be a chance of him having to show his non-existent cycling skills, he slept like a baby. Majhbeen, who had spent the morning after the function separating peas for phupho's breakfast, was questioning her friendship with Hira.

What happened after was a blur. You know, like you're boiling milk and it is still sticking innocently to the side of the *dechki,* and the minute you start to admire the kitchen wall, the milk boils the life out of itself. In such a blink of an eye or milk boil, Majhbeen stopped talking to Hira, Farhan got involved in the family drama and persuasion of a *watta satta,* and the brothers left for a summer in Australia.

* * *

Rashid's mother had always wanted someone like Majhbeen to be her *bahu.* Majhbeen was obedient, confused and knew little about the outside world. At least that was how she had initially been. Her mother-in-law had known that for her autistic son, who was merely a helper to the army, Majhbeen was a golden key. Even when Majhbeen had found out that her husband stammered, forgot things, believed in *parian* and imitated his narcissistic, former wife-insulting father, she did not mind. You see, Majhbeen had fallen in love before. The one-sided, purest and unconditional kind, and she knew that she couldn't feel that way for anyone again. And thus, it didn't occur to her how much lesser she had settled for. And to be very honest, she hadn't led a spectacular life to have standards to look up to; a simple being with simple thoughts, she was.

Three days after the wedding, Rashid had come out of the room, running like he was on fire with his legs and arms flailing all over the place. "My wife's a snake," he had said. For the next few hours, he had a high fever and slowly with Majhbeen covering his forehead in napkins soaked in ice-cold water, he had been told that it had all been a bad dream. After that, Rashid's ami also taught him to not be scared of the wife, but to scare her instead. "Keep her in your *muthi.*" she said. "What you say goes, what she says doesn't matter." And that's what Rashid did. However, once Rashid started getting posted in different cities, Majhbeen's behavior altered. She started forgetting the *salan* on the stove, till it burned to a crisp, and she started putting the clothes on spinning mode three times in a row, and she started eating like a lunatic. Rashid's mother had lived her life in Shampur, a small *kasba* where everyone would sleep before *shaam,* hence its name, because a *pichal-peri* would knock on the doors, asking for gold. She had realized that her *bahu's* behavior was rather unnatural. And the last straw was when she saw Majhbeen offering *namaz,* by tying her hands backward, rather than on her chest, and for *sujood,* putting her head between her legs whilst standing. She hadn't been afraid of her *bahu,* for she had seen stranger things. But, she had ended up calling Majhbeen's father, threatening to have her son divorce his daughter if the truth wasn't told.

"Tell me the truth," she had said. "I know how to deal with these things and I will make her well. But you need to tell me what has happened to her. If you do not, or if you trick me, she will be sent back."

Startled, guilt-stricken and thankful for the hope that had just been promised to him, Majhbeen's *abu* had told Rashid's *ami* everything.

* * *

A thin streak of sunlight, with particles dancing up and down, fell on Mohsin's face. It was as if he was playfully being told to wake up. The tiredness had passed, but the strain from the day before remained. He rubbed his eyes and sat up. Looking at the unfamiliar wall paint, and feeling the cold marble floor beneath his toes, he recalled that he had spent the night in Hira and Farhan's house.

After splashing his face with water (only enough to force open his eyes), he stepped outside. Zaryab was already seated in the lounge, and the moment he saw Mohsin, he placed his water bottle down and stood up.

"Good, you're awake. I tried waking you earlier but it was like you were dead or something."

"Yeah, I guess I slept well."

"Pick up your jacket or whatever you have, and let's leave *forun.*" Zaryab said. "Don't ask me anything right now. Just do as I say."

Mohsin stared at his brother and raised his eyebrows. "Did baba call? Or did Zulifqar bhai mess up something at the site?"

"No."

"Then?"

"Baat kyun nahin samaj rahe?" Zaryab lowered his volume, the anger still palpable in his tone. "I can't say anything now. Farhan has gone to the doctor. This is the perfect time to leave."

"Is- is Hira alright?"

"Hira is home. He's gone to bring the doctor home. Stop asking so many questions, dammit!"

Mohsin frowned. "I will leave when Farhan is back. We can't possibly leave Hira or the house alone. *Thori aqal karo bhai.*"

Zaryab walked over and roughly pushed his brother into the guest room. The mole next to his snot-nose quivered, and the supple smooth skin shivered like it was a carpet being vacuumed. Moshin realized that Zaryab was more worried than angry, and thinking that it was in his best interest to leave, he started picking up his belongings.

"Should we tell Hira that we're leaving?" he asked. "It's only polite that-"

"No."

"But bhai, she has to lock the door yaar. She's alone."

"She's not alone."

"But you just said that Farhan has-"

"Majhbeen hai us ke saath, pata nae."

"W-what?" Mohsin quivered. "Majhbeen's here?"

"Why did you stop walking?" Zaryab inquired. "Dekho, you won't listen aisay. There's something wrong with Hira and you're not a doctor neither am I. I'm starting the car, khud aa jana."

Saying that Zaryab made his way out the door.

"I-I'm coming in two minutes," Mohsin replied.

Mohsin brushed off the Lays crumbs on the couch and sat on it. He needed a moment to collect his thoughts. 'I'll say *Allah hafiz* to Hira and leave,' Moshin thought. 'There's no harm in that. I don't know what's gotten into bhai.' He had just thought that when Hira's door creaked and slowly opened on its own. It was like one of those childhood times when Mohsin had spent the lessons at school wondering about Maggi noodles and the moment he'd come home, *ami* had given him some as if she had read his mind.

Mohsin knocked, and when he received no reply or maybe he thought he heard a sniff, he walked inside. The room was awfully cold, it wasn't like air-conditioned *wala* cold, it felt like Naran's roaring wind was gusting on Mohsin's face. Sitting on the bed was Hira, and her arms and legs were tied to the bed's poles with colorful *dupattay*. Her silky hair covered her face, and soft moans could be heard. "Mohsin," she sniffed, "please *mujhe khol dou.*"

Chapter
10

The End

Mohsin looked at Hira. Her eyes pled innocence but her voice seemed dark, and well, not hers. The room was icy, but sweat could be seen pouring down her dimpled chin.

"Cold shivers…" she said, reading Mohsin's mind. "It happens when I get feverish."

Mohsin's stomach churned, and his throat felt dry; things which happened when his body sensed danger; things that had happened when Sheryar bhai had fallen on his foot.

"Mohsin," Hira implored, "please, untie me."

Had he not gotten the odd sensations and warnings, Mohsin would have untied Hira in an instant. "What is this?" he inquired. "Some sick kinky game that Farhan is playing?"

A grin appeared on Hira's face and slowly turned upside down. "He hurts me." she whimpered. "He's

112

hurting me, can you not see?"

"F-farhan would never do that."

"He's tied me up. He abuses me. He hits me."

"S-stop it, Hira. Farhan is not like that. He'd never lay a hand on you."

"But can you not see I am tied?" Hira said, with her lower lip quivering.

"Do you remember what you told me about that *shaadi wali raat?* What happened when you were taking phupho's pins out?" Mohsin asked, suddenly changing the topic.

Hira sat up straight with her arms still held back. Amused, she blew the baby hair strands away from her eyes and looked right at Mohsin. "Oh…I remember." she said. Her voice sounded auto-tuned, and her face appeared free from all worries. "Tell me more."

"You said that you felt odd when the insects came out. And you wanted to recite Bism-"

"Lalalalalala la la la la," Hira cut in. *"Kya huwa jo lari chooti, jeewan ki gaari.."*

"Why are you singing?"

"I like singing!" she chuckled in delight.

"You're not you!" Moshin said, with all the courage he had. He had seen things all his life, but had never talked to them. "Bismillah."

Hira moaned in happiness. "That smack felt good." Her caramel brown eyes turned whitish-gray and she moaned again. "You have a gift."

"I am not here to talk to you. Whatever you are, do not hurt Hira. She does not deserve this."

"Ah, look at you being all pious!" Hira chuckled. "Untie me and I will leave her. *Waada.*"

Mohsin felt bile rising up his throat. "I don't feel so well," he said. "I should go."

"Coward."

"Calling me names won't make me stay."

"You've always been a coward."

"And you're right…" Moshin replied, "I am not pious. This is why I cannot set you free or be of any help."

"Are you going to return to that brother who doesn't care for you?" Hira giggled. "Coward."

Mohsin shrugged. "Goodbye."

"You're such a coward that you couldn't take a stand for me." came a voice from behind him.

Mohsin turned around at once. "Majhbeen?"

"I loved you. I fell in love with your art. Your soul. And you promised that together we'd be the happiest." Hira mimicked Majhbeen.

"Stop it! She couldn't possibly have told you this. It was between us and only us!"

"We had a summer romance, purer than any other. You loved my simplicity and you pledged to me the world. But for me, you were the world."

"Screw you! *Bakwaas!* This is bullshit!" Mohsin yelled. "You don't know about anything that happened between Majhbeen and me. Nothing. Nada. Zero!"

A tear strolled down Hira's plump red cheeks. "You made me believe it was one-sided," she said in Majhbeen's high-pitched voice. "You stepped back and let me be. You forgot it like we forget bad days. Why did you do that Mohsin?"

"I need to stay calm. This isn't Hira. You're some demon who can read my thoughts. But the truth is that you don't know jack shit. If you knew, you'd know that Majho is happy with Rashid."

"Say that to make yourself feel better," Hira hissed and twisted. "Coward, you are!"

Shivering, Mohsin made his way out the door.

"Suraj huwa madham...chand dhalne laga." Hira's melodious voice could be heard outside the house.

Zaryab was in the parking lot talking to Farhan with a shopper of medicines swinging from his arm.

"Well…" Farhan said while looking at Mohsin. "Your bhai tells me that you're leaving. I'm sorry *chai pee kar gapshap nahin kar sakay.* We will surely do it another time."

"Bhai can leave." Mohsin said. "I'm not leaving."

"Stop being so childish, Mohsin." Zaryab replied, clearly annoyed. "Farhan needs to take care of his wife. Why are you being-"

"I am finally going to stop being childish," Moshin blurted. "I look up to you bhai but this is wrong. We all know that medicines cannot cure Hira.."

"That's not true!" Farhan blurted. "These are the imported ones, *yar."*

"It's not about the *dewai,* for God's sake," Mohsin replied. "We all know that there's something.."

"Something?"

"Something odd about her. Something linked to phupho or Majhbeen and that day. We need to *help* her!"

"Oh alright." Farhan replied. "Allah-hafiz. Once the medicines work, I'll call you."

Zaryab pushed Mohsin towards the car door. "Sit inside." he said, "It's an order."

"Bhai he has Hira tied with bloody *dupattay!* He can't cure her like this!" Mohsin gulped.

"What the hell are you on about?" Farhan said, stopping. "Do you want me to get you some medicine too?"

"Allah *kasam!"* Mohsin replied. "She's in there, bhai and she's tied up!"

Zaryab glowered. He then brushed back his hair and

made his way to the house. Farhan followed him.

"Why are you waiting outside now?" he said to Mohsin. *"Andar aao aur hume dikhao."*

There had been very few incidents in Farhan's life that had startled him. He had always been a man very much in control of his emotions and somehow, nothing really bothered him. However, what he saw that day, made his feet tremble, and his soul shake. He felt like he was a grain of salt in his ami's salt shaker and she just wouldn't stop shaking it.

His wife sat on the fan, going round and round, with her shoulder dislocated and two of her front teeth missing. Her clothes were half torn and on the bed was a cluster of plucked eyelashes – her eyes seemed painfully bruised and pink.

She saw the men and smiled, and then without speaking, resorted back to counting her fingers.

* * *

An hour had passed, and the boys sat in Farhan's lounge. Zaryab was the least interested, however, since Mohsin had refused to leave, he had agreed to babysit him till they could find a solution. Farhan appeared to be partially sad, maybe very sad, but it didn't show, which was good because it enabled him to *think.*

They had tried reciting *surahs,* all the ones they knew, but it had made whatever was in Hira, hurt her more. In the last few minutes, she had already ruthlessly clipped her toenails, which she had then eaten.

"We don't have an answer to this." Mohsin replied. "But Majhbeen, her phupho or uncle might."

"We can't possibly drive to Pindi." Farhan replied. "Stupid Majhbeen's phone is switched off, we don't know her whereabouts and we haven't seen phupho in five years. What if she doesn't live in Canal View anymore?"

"We can try."

"Uncle lives in Rehman Gardens, no?" Mohsin continued. "Where the function was held. Majhbeen *ka ghar*. We can go there."

"What if it has nothing to do with them?" Zaryab asked. "What if it's some jinn who just went *ashiq* on your wife?"

"Can jinns do that?"

"Of course." Farhan replied. "Jinns have no rulebook but you yourself said that prior to Mohsin waking up, you saw Majhbeen in that room and Hira talked to Mohsin in Majhbeen's voice and years back she saw a naked phupho. It is somehow linked."

Shortly after, Mohsin, who had suddenly become the decision-maker, a role he had never played in his life, decided that it was better to act than to discuss. Uncle's house was minutes away and there could be no harm in going there talking to him. Zaryab was told to stay with Hira to which he quite bluntly disagreed. "I'm not staying with a jinn!" he said.

"You didn't believe in jinns until a minute ago." Farhan replied.

"I have always believed in jinns." he answered. "I just never thought I'd witness one."

"What if she has a mental illness?" Farhan gulped. "We can't rule out that possibility."

"An overnight mental illness that lets you move things with your mind and speak of secrets no one knows about? Yeah, right."

"We're arguing again," Zaryab said. "Let's just lock her and leave."

"Is locking her a good idea?" Farhan hesitated. "I mean.."

"It's better than taking her with us. Not that she'll happily agree." Zaryab answered sarcastically.

"Okay.." Farhan said. "It hurts. Looking at her hurts. Let's just go."

They didn't know if uncle would be home, or even if he'd be alive. A sheet of dark blue had spread itself on the skies, and the weather had gotten harsher, with strands of thunder making its way to the ground as if it was preparing the boys for the storm that lay ahead.

Uncle *was* home. He himself opened the door. He had gotten shorter- bent to be precise- and his hair had fallen. His breath smelled of blueberries, which was enough to tell the boys that they had come at the wrong time. But, seeing them made him smile, and he welcomed them inside.

"No one comes by anymore." he said. "I've kept cats. But I forget to feed them."

"There's a *tandoor* nearby…" he continued. "I can order food from there."

"No *takaluf,* uncle jee." Mohsin said. "We're here because of a problem."

Uncle sighed. "The problems never end do they?"

They went to the messy lounge, and it all came back at once- phupho's wedding, the tent, the people and the paper flowers.

"This may sound odd uncle but all of it is true and you may not know anything, but.."

Mohsin's voice trailed off. "Nothing is strange to me." uncle said, his alcoholic breath entertaining Mohsin's nostrils.

And so, Mohsin began the tale. He spoke about what he had seen his entire life and what he had seen that day, and more alarmed than uncle was Zaryab who realized how little he had known about Mohsin. He talked about

Majhbeen rather fondly, so much so, that uncle realized how little he knew of his daughter's interests, and then, he told him about Hira, a woman he intended on saving, which made Farhan think that he had never been enough.

Uncle burst into tears and hugged them. "I know everything." he said. "I know more than what you have told and if I tell you, it will deeply hurt you. But, I have hurt many and if you forgive me, maybe God will forgive me."

The three looked at each other, surprised to say the least. They had come to ask about his daughter's whereabouts and his sister's marriage, but little had they known that the day would unfold into more surprises; awful ones.

It started raining outside, after which uncle rubbed his eyes, and the words started to flow from his mouth, like he had rehearsed the tale over and over again, and had waited a long time to tell them the story. As if he had known that they'd arrive.

"It all started when Majhbeen was young," he said. "She went to a park one day, or a *sehan*. I do not recall. I don't know what happened there, because I was never involved in her life, not even when she was a child. She saw things, and she spoke about them but to us, it was a young girl talking with her silly imagination. She had met with a jinni who had been banished from the Himalayan mountains by its tribe for having wronged them. Demonic the jinni was, demonic the jinni is. She stuck to Majhbeen like glue and when her phupho found out, she tried day and night to get rid of her. She succeeded in banishing her from being near Majhbeen, with *wazaif* and *parhae,* only a person who so immensely loved Majhbeen could perform. The jinni went after her- my sister. Made her life *jahanum.* In the morning she'd

119

be Majhbeen's phupho and at night, she'd be Yalooli, the jinni as she called herself. For years, my sister would wake up in cold sweat, with blood on the sheets, like a *Japani* flag, and she would fall sick for weeks in a row. But she loved Majhbeen so much. The molvi and *aalim* who had given up on Majhbeen, gave up on my *bhen* and said that Yalooli would go away if she'd marry. So we tried and tried till finally, Sheryar married her and stayed with her until her death.."

"Phupho is dead?"

"She died a year ago during childbirth. She had started seeing things. Her *parhae* turned on her." Tears gathered in uncle's mouth, like salty seawater being filled into paper cups by Karachi street children. "And that's when the jinni went back to Majhbeen. I did nothing about it until her mother-in-law called, and told me that she had found out, because she could talk to the unseen. I told her everything and she sent back the jinni to a familiar, the only *saheli* Majhbeen had ever had, Hira, to whom the *sheytaan* had shown itself before too. And I let it. I let it free my daughter."

"I- I don't understand," Farhan inquired.

"In order to free my daughter, I gave what I had of Hira's, an old shawl it was, perhaps a notebook too, and the jinni smelled it, and we burned it, and it freed my daughter."

"You sent a witch to harm my wife?" Farhan shouted. *"Budhe, kitni izzat ki teri, tu kaabil hai izzat kay?"*

Mohsin sat him down. He didn't calm him, for the brothers hadn't ever seen Farhan speak out of any emotion, and they themselves hadn't had any time to digest what uncle had just told them.

"I am your *gune-gar.* I am everyone's *gune-gar.* Sheryar is mute now, and I am to blame for it. I am to blame for everything."

"Now's not the time to repent," Mohsin said. "We need to know how to help Hira."

"I-I don't know," uncle stammered. "The jinni is a leech. It needs a body for a body. It doesn't end. It is two hundred years old. Hira needs to fight it out of her, and you, you need to banish it. It cannot be done in days – maybe years..."

"For fuck's sake.."

"Farhan, don't worry. Let's go *abhi!*" Mohsin said. "Now that we know, time is precious."

"My wife's a weakling…" he said. "Fight a jinni? She can't stand a cockroach!"

"She's strong."

The boys left, and before doing so, Farhan held uncle by his collar and threw him across the couch. "I'm sorry," the old man wept. "I'm *so so* sorry."

"You're horrid, drunk and you'll burn in hell," Farhan replied.

Farhan had not felt so strongly before and so, he had acted out. He felt as if he was to blame, for never opening up enough to Hira. He felt like she shouldn't have been left alone, not that day, not ever. He felt like crying, but he couldn't, and that made him shatter the flamingo statue outside uncle's unkempt house. However, the shattering stone bird was just the start of a lot more shattering to come. For when the boys reached home, and opened Hira's door, her lifeless body hung from the fan, with one of those *dupattay* she had been tied with before – red with blue sequins. She had killed herself, for Farhan had been right about his wife, she was a weakling.

Chapter
11

Endings Are Often Beginnings

There is no end until you're in heaven or hell, but that too is the end to your worldly life, and the start of the life thereafter. So technically, there *is no end.* But let's assume we're on about this life, our body and the soul stuck in it, then the end is till this mud made body closes its eyes with clumps of soil covering it and the other bodies around us mourning. That's somewhat an end. When stories end, it's because pens run out of ink, or the writer suddenly wants to write about how gulab-jamun is made or because that was it to the story; there's nothing really more to it.

It is believed that incompleteness is the key to imagination and sometimes, it is there to keep you away from the truth for the truth is so horrid, that it cannot set you free. But some people are persistent. Look at you, for example, persuading me that you'll have it no other way. You need the end, however dreadfully unpleasant it may be and I'm begging you to let it be. But snobbish you always were, and now here I am, typing what has been.

Blank pages and small paragraphs do not change things. The blue door remains blue and Hira remains dead. Buried deep in the ground, with her *hisaab kitaab* going on. That is all I know, and what I wish, what you should wish too, is for her to walk on the staircase to heaven, like Tom did in one episode of the cat and mouse show, and have the slanty in Paradise. Tastier those will be.

Now that we're on the topic of deaths, uncle died last week. Perhaps on a Sunday, and due to the lockdown or the fact that he wasn't such a nice man, no one came to the funeral. Rashid suspected that his father-in-law had the virus, so he definitely did not go. Majhbeen was allowed to go, and I had expected her to be present, weeping profoundly for the abu she had hardly known. But, she had gotten to know the truth and she had chosen to keep her distance.

Talking about the living is scarier, for one day they'll die too and you'll expect me to write about them. Tell you that they're dead. Gone. Non-existent. Please don't ask me if they're in heaven or hell or what they wore when they died. Some people are dead, waiting for their body to die so that they can freely roam the skies, and make it rain for families on picnic days. Sheryar bhai is one of them. He's a lingering soul, with the devil's mark, madder than we had anticipated. Roams around in a half-torn shalwar, not because he doesn't have a new one but because he likes how the air gets to him through that one hole.

Mohsin, the man who loved, was the one who told Majhbeen everything. But that's not all he told. He told her that he still *loved* her, and that if she was willing, they could go to a foreign land where the 'unfamiliar-ness' would make them feel new. But good girls stay married, and very-good girls understand that summer-time love tales don't work out. So she happily sat next to Rashid, alive and well, knowing that one day, she'll replace attachment with sparks.

There's this NGO scheme. I have forgotten its name. It even has a sub-project to recycle paper. Basically, a place where good deeds happen. Oho, I know you're not interested in charitable works but I'm getting to the story, you are *tou* too impatient. So yes, Farhan works there. He's actually the director of marketing and he's doing well. He's kept a beard and he often forgets to comb it, and sometimes you can see biscuit crumbs on it but the call center girls there find it to be cute. It has been a few months, just two, to be honest, but he's doing well for a mourning husband.

Mohsin's parents already lost a son to constant psychiatric care and the town's molvi who comes for spiritual healing. Maybe he's not lost, but time will tell. So they didn't want to lose the other one and they let him go abroad to art school. Whilst Mohsin is letting art heal him, his brother is quarantined in a room, with regular fits and the ability to climb walls. Yes, Zaryab. They say a jinni is in him. More stubborn than you, refuses to leave. But the molvi says that till Eid, she will. At least for a few days, to visit her tribe.

The End.

The Unwillingly Long Honeymoon of Arooj and Kamil

Sometimes Kamil's body smelled like a newborn's supple skin. Other times it smelled like the local milk powder that comes in a sachet. Either way, Arooj could not help dig her face into Kamil's chest and peck each inch of it. 'Oh, how much I want you right now.' she said and bit her lower lip. Kamil playfully pushed her away and then turned her around and held her between his legs like a child. 'Meri jaan.' he said. 'You know we can't…'

The routine was the same: Arooj would try to seduce her husband in any and every way possible and Kamil would try his best not to give in, at most putting it to rest with a quick kiss. It was not that he did not find Arooj's chocolate brown skin to be appealing or her curves to be soft and pillow-like. He *loved* her, inside out. The truth was the very fact that he *could not do it* with his parents in the same house. The thought of undressing his wife under the same roof as his parents, made him shudder. At first, Arooj had understood because the house was small and its walls very thin, and everyone heard everything. But then there were times when no one was at home except Kamil and Arooj and even then, Kamil could not get past one kiss, thinking that his parents would honk any second. 'I can't have our first time turn into a disaster.' he'd say. 'If you love me, please wait.' And so, Arooj waited. She heard women her age talk about their orgasms and the nights that led to those orgasms, and she felt her heart sink deeper and deeper. When she thought that she could not take it anymore, the sex-less life, she resorted to confiding in a friend; the one that lived seas apart and had no plan of coming to Pakistan and so she thought that her secret would be safe.

'I love him,' Arooj stated. 'And I am sure that he loves me too. He is a darling creature, really. Massages my feet at night, irons his own clothes, takes me out on Sundays to Zouk, and sometimes even talks back to his mother when she gives me piles of undone dishes to do.' There was a brief pause.

'Arooj,' the foreign friend replied. 'I think he is queer.' Now the pause was longer.

'Queer?' Arooj exclaimed. 'But that makes no sense!'

'Queer – as in *gay.*'

'I know what queer means!'

'I bet Kamil bhai likes men. That is the only explanation, my friend. It has been three months and he sleeps next to you without even touching you...'

'He sometimes caresses my hair and pecks my nose...' Arooj cut in.

'That does not count. It is *not you*. It is him. Warna no one in their right mind can claim to be in love with you and not *want you.*'

Arooj was twenty-seven but her prominent, well-defined features made her appear to be a little older than she was. However, despite that, she was very attractive.

She ate clean, went out for walks, and invested in good skincare products. To top it all off, she had been blessed with good genes. 'If he doesn't like me now when I am fitter than ever, I do not know how will he want me in a year or so...' she said. The thought of Kamil not wanting her devastated her and now that there was a possibility that he may never want her, Arooj was miserable. She stuffed her mouth with some Sugar Scoop gelato and a tear rolled down her cheek. 'I shouldn't be eating this...' she mumbled. 'But it is *so* good, perhaps the only good thing in my life right now.'

Kamil was shorter than most men in his family, but his dimples, and eyes the color of emerald instantly drew attention. He had fallen for Arooj the first time he had seen her, even though his sisters had bluntly told him that he could do much better. 'It is her I want.' he had said. 'No one but her.' And he had proudly told Arooj about what he had said. *But at the moment it seemed to Arooj that Kamil wanted anyone but her.*

After four months of their marriage, Arooj started to wake up covered in sweat with a bitter-sweet memory of an erotic dream in the late hours of the night. She would then squeeze her legs together and force herself to sleep. Soon, the dreams increased and so did the frustration. 'I think we both should see a therapist.' she said to Kamil. 'I will not take no for an answer.'

'W-why? Are you depressed?' he inquired.

'I am going to be if you don't accompany me to a therapist.'

The therapist turned out to be a relationship counselor who instructed Kamil to get some physical tests done and come back after. Arooj made sure that they got the results the following evening and came back as soon as the clinic opened. 'Just fix him.' Arooj said when Kamil was not in the room. 'Please tell me that he can be fixed!' she added. The therapist called them both one by one in the room for a good thirty minutes each and then at the end called them in together. 'Well, the good news is that you do not need to come back for a follow-up visit. Kamil is very healthy both physically and mentally and so are you, my dear.' he exclaimed as the spectacles slipped down his oily nose. 'The bad news is that Kamil here is suffering from some sex anxiety. Nothing too big. Nothing at all to worry about. You two need a vacation. Head out to the northern areas for a week or so. I am talking from experience. Things will come back to normal.'

'Every time we need to have sex, we need to make a stop to Murree?' Kamil inquired, clearly confused about the advice that he was being given. 'Maybe some medication...'

'Nonsense. You don't need any medicine. And once you have sex, you will be comfortable doing it in your house as well.' the therapist said.

'Thank you, doctor!' Arooj replied and pushed Kamil out of the room. 'There is no way we are going to Murree. Dubai at most.'

Arooj had been born in France and so for eight years of her life, she had traveled Europe before her family had settled in Pakistan. Kamil on the other hand had never left Lahore except for that one quick overnight trip to Faisalabad to deliver panjeeri to his grandmother.

'Why not Murree?' he asked Arooj. 'The thought of the snowy mountains excites me.'

'That is just what you see in films, oho! Snow in Murree is dirty. It'll spike up your anxiety. Just book a trip to Dubai. A good hotel at Jumeirah. Visa comes in two days. Comfort and fun. If you want, we can skip dessert safari. Don't want you puking on our honeymoon.'

Kamil knew better than to argue with his wife so he took a back seat. Arooj made all the bookings as quickly as she could, and they left for Dubai. 'The plane is crowded.' Kamil said. 'What if we catch Corona?' 'Uff, just wear your mask. Covid or no Covid, just think about the eight nights of endless sex we will have!'

Kamil took a deep breath. He was looking forward to the love-making but the entire process leading up to it was making him tired and anxious. His palms were sweaty and his head was dizzy. However, his worries flew away with the humid Dubai wind when he reached the hotel: everything was spectacular. No one came in without knocking, there was no child jumping on the bed, the room smelled like roses and freshwater, and there was no window. 'It is like they designed this for people to have sex!' Kamil said excitedly. Arooj rolled her eyes. She was tired; tired of the flight, tired of the multiple rapid tests, and tired of having married a child.

Arooj's tiredness wore off as soon as Kamil's anxiety did. After a warm bath and even longer foreplay together, they made sweet love on the white sheets. The silence was promising, Arooj's breath gave the aroma of coconut and honey, which made Kamil imagine that he was having a glass of pina colada on a tropical island. Their bodies slid against each other so very smoothly, and they orgasmed at the same time. 'So, this is what heaven is,' Arooj panted. 'This is what I had been missing out on for months.' She clung to Kamil like a long-lost friend for the remaining night.

'I am so thankful that you're not gay!' Arooj laughed the next day at breakfast. 'Best feeling in the world.'

Before flying, they had made a plan for each day: the Dubai Mall, the fire show, the 2020 Expo, the global village, a one-day trip to Abu Dhabi, and an entire list of eateries they needed to try. Arooj intended to go everywhere In a taxi because the last thing she wanted was Kamil's OCD going off in a metro with a night resulting in no sex. *But,* none of what was planned happened. The couple stayed in the hotel with casual walks to the beach at night and at all times they were not eating, they were doing the deed. 'This *is* the perfect honeymoon!' Arooj gasped as she lay next to her husband. 'You take me to a new place every time we do it!'

On the seventh day, the couple paid the hotel to get the covid test done on the premises. Then they went out to grab some breakfast and head back to the hotel. Since they took a stop at the beach and rolled on top of each other on the sand, they returned almost at lunchtime with a steamed dumpling takeout and a half-eaten slice of pecan cheesecake. As they head towards the elevator with the trail of sand grains following them, they were stopped by the receptionist. 'Room 102?' she asked, fixing her mask. 'Follow me, please.'

'I think we ruined their carpet,' Kamil whispered. 'Should have washed ourselves.'

The couple was led to a small room and were asked to be seated at a distance. 'I am afraid that your wife has tested positive for the virus.' the receptionist said. 'We have informed the authority and they will come within an hour or so to take her to the quarantine center.'

Arooj was dumbfounded. 'What! It could be a false positive! There are so many people who get that. I have no symptoms! I- please check again!'

'I am sorry madam, there is nothing we can do. The test has also been emailed to you.'

'Wait' Kamil instructed. 'Let me talk.'

'I know the protocol.' Kamil continued. 'But can she not quarantine here instead? This way we will be able to test in a day or two to rule out the possibility of it being a false positive. But if you send her to the quarantine center, they won't let her test till the sixth day and honestly, I have missed so much office work.'

'I cannot help.'

'If I could talk to the manager...'

'I *am* the manager.'

Arooj snatched the food from Kamil's hand and started to sob. 'Oh my God!' she wailed. 'Your parents will kill us. We don't even have the money. Oh my God! I still had to purchase some lipsticks. We still haven't bought gifts!...'

'I swear I don't have covid!' she blubbered.

Kamil stepped outside of the room and under the shadow of the artificial tree in the lobby, placed all the money he had in his wallet on the receptionist's lap. *'Please,'* he pleaded. 'I will have my friends wire more money as well. Just let her stay here.'

'There are no rooms vacant.'

'She can stay in room 102. You can shift me to any small place.' Kamil requested. 'You look Pakistani. You can understand.'

'I am Indian.'

'Indian Pakistani friends friends!' Kamil smiled sheepishly. 'Please.'

In an hour, it was settled. Arooj and Kamil were to stay in the same hotel, in different rooms and Arooj was not allowed to leave the premises. She would be tested again on the second night. Their room fare was doubled and the dumplings went cold and soggy.

All Arooj did was take pictures from her room and post them with captions that entailed that they had decided to *enjoy some more* and Kamil transferred his savings for the stay ahead. In his mind, he had always known that good sex would come with a cost.

On the second night, Arooj's result came back positive again, and now no test could be taken till the sixth night. More irked than he had ever been for not providing sex, Kamil shifted to a hotel in a remote area where they decided to quarantine together. The weather there was colder at night, there was no metro station in sight, and it felt a lot like night-time in Faisalabad. The couple survived on street food which surprisingly tasted much more delicious than the meals they had heavily spent on, and Arooj made it clear by repeatedly stating that they were a part of a scam so Dubai people could make more money. 'Because they need money from us, right?' Kamil snapped. With all the time in the world, and the smallest bed they had laid on, the couple did not have sex – the one thing they had come for.

You may now think that Arooj tested negative (finally) and the couple returned to Pakistan but that did not happen. It went something like this: Arooj *did* test negative and they *did* book flights, however, this time, as fate wanted it, Kamil tested positive. The couple returned to the two-star hotel and wept together. 'I will *never* fuck you again…' Kamil moaned. 'You have been so off-putting in the past one week that I will not be asked to be fucked.' came a reply, in-between wails. Kamil felt sick but it was due to the amount of tin iced tea he had consumed and even after a week, he was asymptomatic. Kamil and Arooj tested negative on the 1st of Feb when they reached the airport late and were not allowed to board. Kamil thought that he would have a nervous breakdown and Arooj almost *did* have one. They spent a few hours at the airport till the next flight and reached home without a rupee in their accounts, smelling of sweat, dread, and carrying the flight's sealed water cup with them as if their life depended on it.

With nights that followed, both of them- not one, but both- had horrible dreams. They relived the amazing first few nights of sex, but with a twist. Both of them stood at room 102's door and saw themselves do it. Even though the room had no window and the door had been locked, there stood a few men and women floating in the air with extremely long necks looking at them doing it. They were constantly whispering and one of them even bit Kamil's ear.

Then once when Arooj and Kamil did it in the hotel room shower and had trouble doing so, they saw in a dream that there stood a woman between them with six breasts and both of them could pass through her. Their last and most recurrent dream was of them in the taxi traveling to the *other hotel,* with the long-necked, very smiley, and see-through people sitting on their backpacks and traveling with them.

One month has passed and the nightmares have stopped. The couple has not had sex since their return from Dubai.

The End.

Shaadi Ever After

Chapter
1

Baat Pakki

My heart sank when I looked at Hashim. It felt like all the goodbyes in life had been said at once, like I had stinging worn out *chappals* which I couldn't take off. His beard carried the weight of us, and the plastered smile on his face was the widest that I had ever seen; collecting the air through the space between his teeth so that he wouldn't run out of breaths till night. I saw him chew the *samosa's* crust for a long time and when he knew that no more could be said, he excused himself from the room. I didn't blame him. He had tried. I didn't blame *baba,* he had waited. And I didn't blame myself, for I had loved.

Our story ended before it could start and now that I think of it, it is much like those rupee ten Lays crisps, full of betraying air, with the weight of a few thin promising chips. Hashim was my cousin, my *phupho's* son but you shouldn't remember him like that – he was in fact, a man too romantic for his age, who liked oranges and sunsets and had a degree in art. He *was art.* He smelled of hardships and Comfort fabric softener and I adored how he washed the worries off my palette. It was *dophair* time love, with rooftop meetings and stolen glances and Jazz packages.

We waited for him to complete his education, and then waited for him to attend one of those foreign jewelry design workshops which *baba* funded, then we waited for him to get a job that paid enough for him to wed off his sisters one by one, but then we had waited too long, and *baba* gave his word to his friend's son, who knew about *Hashim* and I, in fact, the first time he introduced himself, he told me how he's *subah,* and how oranges aren't the world's best-loved fruit, and that crafting jewel samples from Maggi isn't a hobby.

My *khandaan* was a strictly conservative one, and *baat pakki* meant a telephone call, a few soggy *chum chums* from Gourmet, and *ami's* tears. But, Nibhaan was a London man, who double ironed his shirts, and his mother was answerable to the entire society she lived in, and so she made a list of functions. There was the *dholki,* the *sangeet,* the mixed-*dholki,* the *mehndi,* the *shaadi,* the *walima,* and the few Gymkhana dinners after that. *Shaadi* main *rakhi firni ki kasam,* I won't lie, I did forget Hashim in the midst of the blinking stage lights and the dancing. But after the lights went off, and I went to my new house with Nibhaan, who insisted that I call him *niboo,* I started weeping for my tragic love story.

We didn't make love on the first night, or the night after that. Nibhaan wanted me to adjust to the idea of him, and his fifty-year-old house, which comprised of us, his mother, his father, *bee jaan,* who was neither his *nano* nor *dado,* and the stray cats that slept in the servant quarter. The doors of the house remained shut most of the time and the insides smelled like old mattresses and boiling white *channay* most of the time.

Uncle was twenty-two years older than aunty which perhaps was aunty's ticket to getting her way around the house. She'd wake up at noon, get dressed and leave with her committee friends who lived in the posh areas of Gulberg. There was no one to clean the house, to run the usual errands and to look after her husband and she told me that it had always been this way, so I didn't have to do anything. But in all honesty, I felt that it was my job to tidy the cushions of the lounge at least, to brush off the dirt on the ornaments, and to ask if uncle needed anything. Uncle never needed anything and only wanted me to sit next to him and hear him tell the stories of his appliances factory on Wahdat road – his most prized possession. He didn't run it anymore, and neither did his son but he had spent more years with the mill than with his wife and so, his eyes lit up with anticipation as he spoke of assembling deep freezers for rich men.

For the first month in the house, I didn't ask about *bee jaan*. I didn't know what her role was in the house, except to steam *channay* and offer some to uncle during noon. As far as I recall, she was always up, and with wide toad-like eyes, eyed everything I did. Her appearance was that of an old woman drenched in worries, and her hair was greasier than the *channay* she made. I occasionally smiled at her and she smiled back, but that was it. I never liked *Bee jaan*. She carried colorful *tasbeehs* in her hand and I would often find her whispering something under her breath and blowing on my clothes. I started placing my clothes in a locked cupboard and one evening I found her sniffing my laundry. According to *ama,* I was thinking too much and that poor *bee jaan,* just wanted company but I had seen enough Indian movies to know those old women who mutter *mantar shantar* are never up to any good.

One night, whilst lying in bed and staring at the *deemak* infested ceiling, I questioned Nibhaan about her.

"Nibhaan," I said. "I want to ask you something if you don't mind."

"Nibhaan-"

"Haan jee. I'm awake. *Boliye."*

"You've never really told me anything about *bee jaan.* I don't know what relation you have with her."

"What do you want to know, *jaan?"*

"Just – who is she?"

"Well," Nibhaan took a long breath. My eyes were fixed on the roof, and my mind was thinking a lot of things at once, one of them being: will the wall slowly decay and fall on me one day or not. But, I knew that Nibhaan's pauses usually meant that he was uncomfortable. Like he had been when I had asked him to do something about the molds on the bedroom walls.

"Well," he continued. *"Bee jaan* is actually my mother. Mama and papa couldn't have a child for eight years. Mama was too little to carry a baby in her womb. At least that is what the doctors said. My dado forcefully married papa to his cousin and papa divorced her shortly after, but I had already made my way into this world-"

I gulped. The information was too much to decipher and just when I had gotten the hang of it, Nibhaan burst out laughing. His egg-yolk yellow teeth glittered and his Adam's apple rapidly moved up and down his neck. His *kehke* made me uncomfortable.

"Kya hou gaya hai yaar," he chuckled. "You're so gullible. *Matlab, kuch bhi. Bee jaan* is papa's *dour ki rishtedar.* Her only son died in a car crash and since then she's been a part of the family."

"Oh," I sighed. "Funny."

I faked a smirk and switched off the night lamp. Nibhaan wasn't funny at all.

I fell asleep and dreamt about Hashim and long blades of shiny grass surrounding us in a rice field. We were so happy, and the sun shone in the mightiest manner as if to welcome us and celebrate our togetherness. Suddenly, the sky began to darken, and a chilly wind blew Hashim miles away. The grass grew longer till I could see nothing but wilting green, and I started to run. Everywhere I went, I stepped on chickpeas, and a crackling sound of a woman's laughter followed me. I saw an unfamiliar face of a woman my age who started to levitate in the air and follow me. The strands of grass sliced my skin and blood oozed out of my cheek.

I woke up to find myself sweating profusely, out of breath and trembling. It took me a moment to catch my breath and regain my senses. I turned on the lamp with a shaky hand and saw Nibhaan lying next to me, snoring peacefully. The bed under me felt damp and I got up to check if my perspiration had gotten the better of me. I jumped off the mattress and straightened my *kameez*. The alarm clock was striking thirteen. Under me was a dark maroon splotch of blood, on the white Chen One Linen. Thinking that I had gotten my period, I checked my trousers but they were dry, and the only moisture between my legs was that of sweat. I examined the blood on the bed by touching it. The red transferred to my finger and it, in fact, was fresh blood. I looked at the sheet in horror and saw the blood spreading like water, dying the snowy bed cloth a shade of scarlet.

Chapter
2

Defence Villa

The walls served the purpose of suffocating more than protecting. Covered in layers of floral colored paint, the decaying bricks still made their way through. The tiles had been stepped on for too long, and the house did not appreciate being decorated for the new bride. It was the only house on the deserted street otherwise filled with fruit sellers, which had celebrated its golden jubilee. Its companions had been refurbished over and over again into factories. The house had made it through for fifty-five years and had seen things that wished not to be seen, had heard stories that occurred through the darkest hours of the night, and had been home to Hindu landlords who set their wives on fire. Nibhaan, who cherished the house, carried a list of names with him of the previous owners. That list also had names of people who had owned the house when it was a resort for Aryan soldiers to enjoy their well-deserved break with women who danced to the rhythm of their hearts, and also names of people who owned it when the brothel was destroyed and was just land on which crops did not harvest for years.

But, what mattered to my *baba* the most was that the house was in Defence, and it didn't matter that the area it was nestled in was no longer a part of Defence, but the land of old manufacturing factories and units. The house was called Defence Villa, and it was large enough to house six families, and that excited *baba* enough to make his drooping mustache stand. When *baba* had toured the house before accepting Nibhaan's proposal, he had been out of breath telling us about the number of rooms, and how his *beti* Sajeer, would be the queen of the house and it felt as if a two-year-old boy with flushed cheeks was describing the taste of a newly tried orange lollipop. *Ama* had calculated the cost of giving furniture for every room even if it meant that she had to sell her jewels, but before she could, Nibhaan had politely refused. I was just allowed to bring my essentials.

The house did not need a makeover, it needed to be emptied. The air was heavy and the rooms unwelcoming. I spent the first few weeks exploring the rooms, most of which were locked. Nibhaan said that *bee jaan* opened them up once a year to get them cleaned. Aunty was least interested in the house, and she spent most of her time out of it. Uncle, bedridden, spent his time seeing aunty come and go, and laughing to himself, reminiscing old memories. During the second month of my marriage, the house had played enough tricks on my mind to make me search for a new hobby.

I had seen blood appear on my sheets more often than I had seen the sheets clean. And with the blink of an eye, it would disappear, as if it had been nothing but my imagination. During the first monsoon rain, I ran outside to drench myself in the rainwater, and even though Nibhaan wanted to accompany me, I felt that the *baarish* was just for me and Hashim and that by enjoying it with my husband, it would be unfair to the only man I had ever loved. The clouds were a shade of lavender that day, and it was the most beautiful splash of colors that I had seen in the twenty years of my life. I ran back inside to get my phone, and when I went back, to my astonishment, the sun was out, and the streets, earlier leveled with rainwater, were dry. I called out to Nibhaan, and told him but he said that it never had rained, and he did not recall asking me to let him come outside. Startled, I waited for his yellow teeth to show, for him to laugh, but he had been serious. Curious and disturbed, I walked outside the house in the blinding sunlight, only to step in cold rainwater, puddles of mud and the sight of the September rain everywhere around us, *but* around the house. It was pouring, and within seconds, I was wet, and when I walked to the gardens surrounding the villa, each step dried me. I came back inside, like a washed and dried doll that the house had played with. I slept early that day trying to forget the occurrence like the bad daydream that it was. In the midst of the very same month, I went out to one of the local markets to buy *bhindi,* and make some for uncle. I never liked ladyfingers, and Hashim only used it to paint designs, and Nibhaan was almost never hungry when he came home. No one in the house was ever hungry, and what was eaten was done to stay alive. Very soon, cooking became an excuse to spend the afternoons outside. During one such noon, I happened to pass by a street vendor selling piping hot *jalebis.* The old man was surrounded by children who were celebrating a cricket victory and a girl who had snuck out of college to meet her boyfriend, and each one of them was appreciating the *sheera-covered delights.* I bought a handful and became a part of the group in admiring the *sweet delicacy.* Every time I would purchase vegetables, I would spot the kind man with the *jalebi* stand and get some treats. After some time, we started talking. It was a stranger's talk. He would ask about my day and I would ask about his. He told me how *jalebis* are made and why his are a class apart. One day, he asked me where I lived and I told him about the Defence Villa. As *ghee* dripped down my chin, I saw the color of his face change and his uncomfortable smile ended the conversation between us. For some days, there was just silence but then one day, he asked me if I was the new bride to which I nodded. He said that he had been called by his brother to decorate the house with lights during the festivities. I said that he must be mistaken because I had never seen my *susral* or *susral wale* lit up.

"No one can be mistaken about the Defence Villa *beti.* People run away from it, but I went to it, to assist my brother with the lights. Each time we put them up, the bulbs would fuse. When we started carrying the bulbs with us on ladders, we saw tiny women beneath us shaking the ladder. We were being paid for our *rozi roti,* and so we continued, till my brother's little boy got electrocuted and we took him to the hospital. He told the doctor that someone had forced his fingers into the socket."

I was horrified to hear what the old man had to say. After questioning him regarding the child's health, I took my *jalebis* and walked back home. For quite some time, I had been raving about the delights to Nibhaan and he insisted that I bring him back some over the weekend which was the only time he returned from office before maghrib. On the weekend, just before my husband's arrival, I fetched some treats to give him with *chai.* Now, you must know that the distance of the Sunday bazaar where the vendor usually sits and the Defence Villa is a two-minute walk. I walked quickly to cover the distance so that the *jalebis* would be fresh. I was greeted by two unfamiliar cars, none of which belonged to aunty at the villa's gate. Nibhaan came outside to tell me that his sister had paid an unexpected visit from Dubai. For the very first time, something that he had said made sense, because my family and I were told about Nibhaan's elder sister who had been married off to a computer specialist in the neighboring country. I quickly placed the oily paper packet on the kitchen shelf and entered through the back door. I was thrilled to be meeting someone from Nibhaan's family, because in that house, my only communication happened with *ami jee* over the phone with weak signals. With a few dabs of powder on my face and the bright red lipstick that I unboxed for the first time after *shaadi,* I made my way to the dining room. Before I could meet my *nand,* Nibhaan standing by the door, asked me if the sweets I had bought were enough to be served. I nodded and went to the kitchen.

"You look beautiful," he whispered, as I went and gave a weak pat on my back. I smiled hesitantly. As I emptied the *mithae* in one of the golden dishes, I saw red worms clinging on to the spiral *jalebis.* I gasped in horror and threw the *jalebis* outside. With sticky syrup still on the tips of my fingers, I scampered back inside to inform Nibhaan. Seated on the sofa was a familiar face, chucking in delight after seeing me. I couldn't remember where I had seen her, but I had indeed seen her, of that I was sure. My *nand* pointed towards a bulk of presents packed with shiny paper. *"Yeh meri bhabhi kay liye."* she said.

I then got up to hug her, and her neck smelled like freshly watered grass after which it occurred to me that she was the levitating woman chasing me in my recurring dream in the grass fields. Gulping, I sat on the dusty couch and tried my very best to not show the fear eating me from within. I saw *bee jaan* make her way inside a while later, pushing a trolly with bakery goods and juice. On the very right, I spotted the *jalebis* in a golden dish, which I had thrown away.

Chapter
3

Massi Kalsoom

When I was seven years old, my dado used to tell me about her sister, Noorain-ul-Sahiba. All of us had heard of her, had seen her in photos, but had never met her. She used to live cities apart, in the middle of some mountains, where the sun hardly shone. She wasn't alone; she lived with her husband, Shah-Ullah, and an adopted Kashmiri boy, who she taught the Quran to. Dado said, that when Noor was young, a jinn from a holy Muslim tribe had come repeatedly in her *amo* jaan's dream, asking Noor's hand for marriage. When dado's *amo* had refused, the jinn had understood. It happened so, that the jinn, who was well known in his world, stayed unmarried for years. It would often knock on *amo's* door, and bring gems wrapped in outstanding fabric (which by the way, could fold itself) for Noor. When Noor became a preteen, or as dado said, 'was on her way to becoming a woman', the jinn started appearing in her dream. It would do no harm and would take the shape of a handsome man, or become light, and show Noor the majestic dimensions that existed for *maqhlooq* other than humans. When Noor's *rishta* with Shah-Ullah was fixed, the frequency of the dreams decreased.

"I am bidding you goodbye, Noori." the winds of the night carried the jinn's message. "I have shown you what it is to love, and your human will love you in a way I might not. Your mother is right, for fire and clay can only cause destruction and I will not let any misfortune fall upon you. If you ever need me, your dreams will guide you."

Before the jinn could leave, Noorain-ul-Sahiba requested that it show himself to her and that this much it owed for she too had grown fond of it. The jinn was reluctant, and it said 'I am only beautiful to my kind.' When Noor persisted and scorned the idea of getting married, *amo* allowed to jinn to show itself, and so the jinn did. Dado's *baji* Noor then lost the ability to speak which had come with the shock of seeing the jinn in its truest form. Shah-Ullah, mesmerized by the beauty of his wife to be, married Noor nonetheless and they went far away from the city life.

I recalled dado's story when I saw Nibhaan's sister sitting in front of me. A wild part of me thought that she was a jinn for I had never seen her before, and yet she had appeared in my dream that had haunted me for weeks. I know the thought was absurd, but nothing in that house was normal and this was the only sense I could make of it. When I shared my thoughts with Nibhaan on the night of his sister's arrival, he exposed his plaque-covered teeth, and laughed in the most horrific manner, which caused him to snort, and I looked away in disgust.

"Get out there, take the driver, you have all the time to make up stories." he replied.

"I can't drive and I don't have a driver."

"Take the one mama uses, *yaar.*"

I didn't want to take aunty's driver for many reasons. One, she was always out, and that meant that I could not have the driver. Two, the driver, whose name I still did not know, was eerie. He stayed the night, never took a leave and was hardly served any food. But that was not the unpleasant part. One time, he had dropped me to baba's house right after *shaadi,* and the entire time he had been staring at me with his bloodshot eyes from the front mirror. He had requested baba for a prayer mat at eight in the morning, and according to my helper, who had run away from the quarter, multiple shadows had appeared behind the driver which had gone into *sujood* with him. When the helper had been watching the shadows in amusement, the door of the servant quarter had shut on its own, which had caused *baji* Shameem to frantically dash back to the house.

Khair, there was no further discussion about the driver with Nibhaan.

Every morning, my *nand,* Gul Nawaz, would request me to fix her a fancy breakfast. It started with Nibhaan's *tareef* of my spinach omelet, and then when I, who never did know how to control her mouth, exhibited the other edibles I could create, turned into a feast Gul would want daily. Out of courtesy, I would make a little of everything she wanted; *suji ka halwa,* cinnamon French toast, poached eggs, *aloo tikkis,* and orange juice. She'd examine each, take a small bite on which she'd chew for the longest time, and then, after some appreciation, leave the entire meal in the kitchen. When I complained to Nibhaan, I was told to make a little amount of each but what is littler than one toast and one bowl and one *tikki,* I thought.

Within two weeks, my tiny arms and not so tiny legs felt weak and drained. My sister-in-law was very demanding and picky and other than asking for food, she made no communication. Ama said that this was a good time to tell Nibhaan to get me some house-help and for the very first time since our *shaadi,* Nibhaan did not smirk, snort or refuse. *Bulke,* the very next day, he said that a *massi* would arrive.

I assumed that I'd have to brief the new maid about the house, discuss the pay and inform her about her work, but, Nibhaan said that the woman who was to come was a friend of the villa, and a trust-worthy *massi* that had fed him milk.

"I didn't drink my own mama's milk." he said. "And you think Gul is picky. Massi Kalsoom was the only woman whose breasts I sucked."

Sometimes I wondered if my baba disliked me because he had always wanted a son. He had married me off to the first *rishta* that had come, to show his sister that I was worthy of someone more than Hashim. But baba, did you not know that Hashim's fingers fit into mine, and his smile followed mine, that he was the *sheera* to my *gulabjamun,* and that he was all the colors that I was not.

The only relation that I had with Nibhaan was that of sex, and meaningless sex is nothing but a trade of the body without the soul, wanting to feel the rain without getting wet, and two instruments making music but rotting within. *But of course,* I had to accept the reality which was Nibhaan, his ghastly existence, and his throttling house.

I nodded and I went back to my room. I covered myself in a summer quilt and wept myself to sleep.

The next day, I was awoken by a rhythmic knock on

my door. *Bee jaan* stood outside, and in a low, croaky voice, informed me about *massi* Kalsoom's arrival. She left me in the garden and I wandered about, till I found the massi sitting under the farthest tree. She was a short woman with an evident thyroid problem and twinkling eyes. Her smiling face was promising, and her wet, unkempt hair was loosely covered with a faded green shawl that she kept adjusting. She shook my hand firmly and told me that she had always wanted to see Neebo *beta's* new *dulhaan* and it was an honor for her to work at the Defence Villa again. She sounded almost like baba, if not more excited than he had been. I told her about what Gul required, and that the house didn't need any keeping.

"I had been doing fine." I spoke in an unexpectedly fine Punjabi accent. "I stay in my room and mind my business. No one needs any help. The work has exceeded because of the guest and I wish for you to help me during breakfast."

"Oh *nayi dulhaan,*" she replied. "This house always needs keeping. It's a living being on its own. And I can see that it has missed me. I will keep you and it very happy."

Shrugging, I returned to my room. It was early for me to be up but I did not feel like sleeping again. As I laid on the sofa to rest, I felt a small prick and I jumped right back up. There was nothing sharp on the sofa cloth, but something had pricked me so I zipped the sofa cushion open and just like that, and to my astonishment, with the stuffed cotton were a handful of nails wrapped in yesterday's newspaper. I zipped the sofa back up and waited for Nibhaan to return. I applauded myself for the evidence that I had found. There was something wrong with the house and the people in it, and I could feel it.

The day went by like the previous days. I roamed around the house, listening to old Indian songs, and talking to ama jee. I ironed some clothes and sat with uncle after maghrib to listen to his oddly satisfying life tales. I waited for aunty to return, asked about her day and went back to my room. The entire time had been spent thinking about the nails and the person plotting against me.

Ama said that I looked pale, dull and widowed. She instructed me to get ready for 'Nibhaan' and that seducing him would be the answer to all my wants. I didn't want to 'dress up' for a man I despised, but I had always been an obedient daughter, and so I put on my best clothes – the pink laced *kameez* with the silky brown trouser- and untied my ponytail to let the naturally ironed-sheet-like hair fall on my shoulders. I opened my eye kit and took a hard, long look at the hazel eye lenses.

Hashim loved your lenses. He said that you looked like a French artist's painting with that wheat skin of yours and those artificially colored eyes. Why would you wear these for a man who doesn't tremble when you touch him....

I brushed the thoughts away and forcefully put on the contacts. When I had gift-wrapped myself to be presentable, I walked to the corridor upstairs. There, between locked, dusty rooms was a huge mirror in which I often looked at myself, but today in it, I wanted to examine my dolled up self, head to toe. The light was fused and with the moon's light, there was only so much I could see, but I smiled at my reflection and my atta colored skin.

Itni soft si attay jaise cheeks hain. Goond dun main tumhe.

Hashim's remark rang in my head and I giggled to myself. Suddenly, the entire corridor lit up, and laughter echoed. It felt as if several women with shrill voices had started guffawing. There was a noticeable drop in the temperature which made chills run down my spine, and frightened, I took my leave. As I raced downstairs, something got caught in my left eye and it started throbbing instantly. The pain was excruciating and it made me groan and cry. Gul, who was watching from her room, rushed towards me.

"Sajeer? Are you alright?"

"My-"

Before I could tell her that something had entered my eye, she placed her fingers around my eye and stretched it open. The tormenting ache instantly went away.

"Tha-thank you." I said. "How did you know that something was wrong with my eye?"

"You were twitching it. Uh – it was watery. Watery and red."

I was made to wash my face and lay down in my room. Gul had removed both the lenses and had tossed them in the bin.

"Bad quality lenses, you wear. I'll get you some from Dubai."

But, my lenses weren't the problem. Something had entered my eye and of that I was sure. Nibhaan checked up on me when he returned and instructed massi Kalsoom to massage my head till I slept. I could not sleep because I wanted to tell Nibhaan about my finding and so when the massi left, I turned on the light and went outside looking for my husband. Soft whispers were coming from the closed dining-room door. I had been taught to not disrupt ongoing conversations and knock, and so I thought that I would wait.

"What happened to her?" Nibhaan's voice came from behind the door.

"Bhai, I think that she was meddling around. *Gusah aa gya hou ga unko.*"

"*Aisa kyun keh rahi ho Gul?*"

"She was maundering upstairs."

"Upstairs?"

"*Haan.* Upstairs. *Bee jaan* tells me that she often goes upstairs. *Aj tou tyaar ho kar gae thi.* When she came back downstairs, a *jinn ka bacha* was swinging with her and had its thumb in her eye. *Wou tou maine usay guseh say dekha tou wou bhaag kya.*"

"Oh. *Samjhata houn isay.*"

"*Theek hai.* Get her a new pair of lenses, *wesay. Mera khayal hai apke liye tyaar hoyi thi.*"

The conversation ended and I could hear footsteps approaching the door. The sound of the soles against the floor matched my fast beating heart – which I thought would pop out of my chest. I silently tip-toed back to my room and hid under my bed. With shaky, sweaty fingers, I started to dial ama's number. I had to get out of the house.

Chapter
4

Khush Khabri

I sat with ama and Gul in the villa's bedecked lounge silently. Massi Kalsoom had just served ama *chai,* and aunty had churlishly excused herself from the lounge. Baba and Nibhaan were seated in uncle's room, discussing the entire issue because 'men know better', and in all honesty, I just wanted to pack my bags and run back home, even if it resulted in baba's *narazgi.*

This wasn't the first time I had resorted to calling my parents. Back in seventh grade, I had out of sudden emotion, slapped a classmate for spreading rumors about me having a boyfriend. This had resulted in a suspension letter, and I had called ama to have a talk with Alishba's parents to apologize on my behalf – which according to the principal was my only way out. When I was in Kinnaird College, I had bunked many math lectures, which, again, was not entirely my fault because numbers made me feel dumb, and my *dour kay* chacha had caught me sipping a

156

strawberry milkshake at the McDonalds nearby. His exact words had been: *Main ami abu ko phone karoun yah ap?*

But today, I hadn't called ama baba out of *jazbaat,* I had called to inform them that my sanity was in danger, because of the house and the people nestled in it. I hadn't unlocked the bedroom door for Nibhaan till baba had shown up at the villa. After which I had wept hysterically, telling them everything in between sobs. There were no iron nails found in the sofa, and Gul swore on the Quran that she had seen no jinn's child clinging to my ear, and Nibhaan had looked at me with utter disappointment. But of course, I had insisted and had mentioned the odd behavior of each one of them, including what the *jalebi* vendor had told me.

Gul waggled her eyebrows and followed massi to the kitchen. Finding alone time, ama finally spoke up.

"Beta, " she said. *"*It takes time. *Ghar bnana parhta hai.* It's a woman's job. You're *tou* so lucky. *Na saas ka pressure aur na hi sussar ki rouk touk.* Gul is a guest and she'll leave shortly. I fail to understand what problems you have. Your problems aren't even real problems. *Wou Aneela ki beti ka husband usay marta hai. Saath wali Shaista hai na,* she blames her *bahu* for not having a son. And you, you sit on the bed each day and have McDonald's."

I looked at ama in disbelief. I was pretty sure that Gul was standing behind the wall eavesdropping, and after having cried like a child for hours, I had no words left to utter.

"Problem *hou jaye gi."* I replied. *"Keh tou rahi houn,* nothing over here is fine."

"Dekho Sajeer, if you feel scared *tou* stop seeing those Netflix shows of *angreaz* kids and monsters. *Apke* baba *say keh kar subscription cancel karati houn.* No one asked you to roam upstairs alone. You see foolish stuff, then you

imagine things and then you create trouble for us. *Kya sochta hou ga* Nibhaan?"

Nibhaan nay kya sochna tha. He was the strangest of the lot. He was probably going to be careful next time or maybe, there wasn't going to be a next time.

"The show you're talking about is Stranger Things *ami,* and it has nothing to do with all this. *Har baat main Netflix aur phone ko kyun lay atien hain?"*

Ama sipped her tea and shook her head. *"Har baat per behas."*

At that point, I had realized that whatever I was going to tell her would have been in vain. She was blinded by baba's *baatein,* and Nibhaan's manipulative attitude. I knew that if I kept going, the conversation would turn to my inclination towards Hashim, like it always did and we both did not want that.

"Hashim is getting married." ama spoke up. I guess, my mother *had been waiting to talk about it.* Her following silence indicated that she had taken the news well and that she intended for me to do the same.

"Your *phupho* will probably just invite us on the walima. She *tou* didn't even tell us about the *rishta.* Mehmoona *ayi huwi thi,* she told me. Society *ki hi larki hai. Itne well off tou nae hain. Chalo, hume kya.* We're *tou* happy you got wedded at such a great place. *Aisay rishte ab kahan milte."*

My heart sank. I knew that at one point in life Hashim would have gotten married, it was inevitable, but I wasn't ready for it. I didn't know that it would be too soon. I thought, maybe, just maybe, somehow, I'd leave Nibhaan and baba would marry me to my childhood sweetheart. I deserved that much. An evening from six months ago flashed before my eyes: It was mid April and Hashim was brushing my bristly hair off my forehead. We were in the storeroom going over dado's old albums, thinking that thirty years from now, we'd be doing the same, only we'd be looking for our wedding photos. The funny part was that Hashim had made everyone in the family agree to an underwater photo-shoot, because we *had* to do something different. I had spent nights searching for water-proof makeup on Daraz.

I looked at ama and forced a smile. *"Achi baat hai,"* I replied. "He deserves the very best."

The silence between ama and I was disrupted by baba and Nibhaan entering the lounge, arm in arm. Baba was laughing and Nibhaan was mimicking a politician.

"Chalain begum?" baba asked ama.

"What do you mean?" I interrupted. "I have to pack my stuff *abhi.*"

"You're not going anywhere, *beta.*" baba answered, straightening his mustache. "I have talked to my *damaad,* and he is my *damaad* after all. I believe in him and he will keep you safe and happy. Misunderstandings *hou jati hain.*"

"But baba jee-"

"No buts, *Sajeer.* Nibhaan is your husband. You're his rcsponsibility."

He then looked at Nibhaan. *"Bta dena beti ko."*

Tears welled up in my eyes and before I could say another word, *ama* pinched me from behind. A moment later, we all, including *bee jaan,* who had been Allah knows where for the past few hours, walked ama and baba to the car.

I wanted to run behind the vehicle, or run to the other side where if I kept running, could end up in a new city, country or continent, where both my parents and my husband couldn't find me. Maybe, Hashim had already started running and this was the only way out.

Snapping back to reality, I followed Nibhaan inside. Rather than sitting in the lounge, he took me to the bedroom and sat me down.

"I'm sorry," he said. His face seemed larger than usual, and his tongue occasionally got stuck between the spaces in his lower teeth. "I haven't been a very good husband. We never got time to ourselves, just you and I. And so, uncle and I have decided that it is best for us to spend some time together. Alone."

The very last thing that I wanted was to spend time with him alone. I had tried to get to know him, I had cooked for him, cleaned after him, and tried to love him if that even made sense, but I had always been repelled by his existence.

"Sajeer, *jaan,*" he continued. "I will book the tickets tonight. We will go to Thailand next week. You'll love it. *Pehle* Bangkok *jayein gay.* I'll take you to the best seafood restaurants. Then we will go to *Pattaya,* and lay down under the sun. Just you and I – and then I will make sure that all your tensions are resolved."

"Thailand?"

"*Jee,* Thailand."

I will be lying if I say that my eyes did not light up at that very moment. I had never been out of Pakistan. We had been too middle-class to even avail our PC Bhurban membership and I had never been on a plane. Just the sound of Thailand sounded exotic to say the least.

"Are you happy now?" he inquired.

"Yes." I replied. "I am happy."

The next day was a busy one. I went to the passport office with Nibhaan, to get my very first passport made. For the first time since *shaadi,* aunty sat down with me to tell me about her trip to Thailand. She told Nibhaan to take me to Phuket instead of Pattaya, and she asked me to bring her coconut oil. She then asked Gul to take me shopping for my five day trip.

"Thai women have smooth skin. Even makeup bounces off it, and it is because of the oil that they use." she said.

"*Baji...*" Massi Kalsoom uttered in excitement whilst straightening my sheets. "*Mulk say bahir ja rahi hain, meray liye na sahi, ghar kay liye kuch zaroor lana.*"

I chuckled sheepishly. "Jee."

Massi Kalsoom was an odd being. She spent her days cleaning every corner of the villa and decorating it. The metal pieces with stone ashtrays were drowned with freshly plucked flowers daily and with the little money she had, she had gotten ornaments from the Sunday bazaar to put in uncle's room. She was obsessed with taking care of the house. Pampering it. *Treating it like a real-life, living human being.*

I thanked God for the sudden plan because if it hadn't been for the planning to Thailand, I would have indulged myself with the sadness of Hashim's *shaadi*. But now I could post a picture of Nibhaan and I on a sunny beach and pretend to be happy. Maybe, like those Juila Quinn novel couples, we too could have a love story.

Shopping with Gul taught me patience. Each time I looked good in an outfit, she'd feel that I was 'showing too much' or that 'I was showing too little.' And eventually, I got to hear that in Dubai, 'clothes are better.' I got a hold of some shirts from Outfitters, but when Gul was in the restroom, I snuck into Mango and purchased my dream jumpsuit. I would be wearing it on the beach picture I'd upload on Facebook for my *khandaan* to see. *For Hashim to see.* The change of thoughts made me believe that I too, at one point had become my mother.

Before Nibhaan and I left for Bangkok, ama and baba

came to the airport.

"Dekho, kitni khush hai meri beti," ama said. *"Wesay bhi,* Hashim would have only taken you to Murree."

Little did ama know that Murree with Hashim wouldn't have been short of a fairytale.

During the plane ride, I woke Nibhaan up. But then when I realized that it would just ruin the sudden 'quality time' that we were spending, I apologized and let him go back to sleep. I felt that the 'house' had followed us because no matter how excited I got, there was a sinking feeling in my stomach. But the truth was that I wanted to switch places. Outside the window, on the wing of the plane, just on the edge, sat *bee jaan,* flying with us, continuously staring at me, eating *channay* with her left hand, and clinging on to the aircraft with the right one. I knew that it wasn't possible. She couldn't possibly be on the wing, but each time I looked, she was there. At first, her hair had covered her face, but when the plane had shifted its position, and the hair had blown off the woman's face, I had realized that it was *bee jaan*. I read *ayat-al-kursi,* turned my head and went to sleep.

I dreamt that the plane stood still, and that little dwarfs fell from the sky and entered it. They slowly spread my legs apart and planted a seed inside. Lying next to me was a goat with its legs apart as well, and the dwarf accidentally planted a human baby seed in the goat but before I could tell it that the goat baby was inside me, they stitched me up and vanished in thin air. When we reached Suvarnabhumi airport, I felt dizzy and Nibhaan took me to the toilet. He handed me a water bottle because there weren't any Muslim showers. Apparently, for *cheeni meeni loug,* a tissue was enough. When I sat down to pee, I saw that the upper part of my vagina had been *stapled* together with a funny string.

Chapter
5

Jinn-in-Law

The Bangkok sky wasn't any different than Pakistan's. It was a shade of polluted blue, and instead of street beggars there were hookers on the roadside. We stayed at Nana Street, which was known for *astagfirullah* reasons, and initially, I thought that it was because Nibhaan would enjoy the view, but he clung on to me, and we arrived at our Grand Five hotel, located above a McDonalds. The coquettish Thai women wore small skirts that exposed their unclean tattooed knees, and they smirked at the sight of their prey. A part of me wanted them to have him, but the other part felt good, because the women flung their breasts playfully around him and whilst my eyes were on their bouncing balls, Nibhaan's were solely focused on the ground. Usually, honeymoon couples go to the islands in Langkawi, but here we were at a traditional bachelor spot, trying to find romance.

The moment we arrived at the hotel, I locked myself

in the washroom. I wanted to examine my vagina; take a long, hard look at the unexplainable stitches that I had magically gotten through my slumber on the flight. I had to conceal them or give a believable excuse to my husband for he had been keen on undressing me right after we had unpacked. It was night time, and because we were tired, Nibhaan was ordering dinner in the room. When I lowered my pajamas and took a bird's eye view, I was taken aback. There was no string, but a dissolved mark, that appeared to be a thread within my skin. As hours passed by, it became a faded marker line that Nibhaan did not notice. Although, when I bent down, my lower stomach felt tighter than usual.

After midnight, we decided to go out for a walk. I had been told that the nights in the alleys of Thailand were forever young. The scene that I witnessed outside was different than when I had arrived. The fruit shops had shut down, and sex toy shops had come to life. The men who were shouting the rates of Durian were replaced by men with naughty eyes displaying gigantic dildos. I shrugged and moved along. We stopped outside a 7-eleven to buy some fried shrimp.

"You like seafood, don't you?" Nibhaan questioned, looking at me in an amusing manner.

"Very much." I answered, slurping down the tangy sauce that came with the coated delicacy.

"Crabs *bhi pasand hain?*"

I nodded. *"Sab kuch.* I've never tried octopus, but I've heard that the tentacles stick to the throat and it's a *muzay ki feeling."*

Nibhaan smiled. *"Chalo,* kal we'll have octopus."

He kept looking at me. "It's just that I've never seen you eat before."

Of course, he hadn't seen me eat before. The only

time I actually ate *paet bhar kar,* was outside that haunted house of ours.

We walked for hours and discussed the weather, the women of Thailand, tax and how many children we should have, all between long, uneasy pauses. I tried to ease into the communication and get excited about the idea of us, and falling in love again, but Nibhaan was an unattractive, mysterious individual. He had the looks of an appealing middle-aged *desi* man and the body of a young boy. The *rishta* aunty had told us about how he was in demand and just because of that, ama had instantly found him to be a *charaag* she wanted her daughter to rub. But, in all honesty, - because I've been as honest as it gets – my *saheli,* Rubab, who I rarely met but uploaded pictures with on Facebook, thought Nibhaan to be her uncle Kamran's look-alike who she found to be drop-dead gorgeous. So, it was safe to think that my inclination towards Hashim might have made me not love my husband. That and the fact that my husband gave me goosebumps.

With seafood breath and breakfast bars, we went back to our hotel. We spent an hour planning for the next few days and then we went to sleep. The next day, after hanging his undergarments to dry, Nibhaan said that he had to talk to me about something.

"It shouldn't worry you, because as far as I know, it *should* make you happy, but *phir bhi,* I thought that I should talk to you about it."

I stopped arranging my clothes and sat up attentively.

"Mama says that husband and wife are like two tyres of a car. Not wheels, but tires. You see, the first wheel is the man, and the second wheel is the woman. But a car can't function like that. Both the wheels need each other, and without the tyre covering, the friction causes them harm-"

I looked at Nibhaan closely. He had a whole lecture

planned, which, by the way, went on for a good half hour.

"So," he continued in between high pitched quotations, "Men and women who are wheels, when are ready for marriage, become tyres, and for the car to be driven, the tyres must know each other's wants, needs, and give each other attention. Most importantly, one tyre should keep the other tyre aware of the changes happening in that tyre's life."

I bit my lip. I wanted to say, *btaa bhi dain.* Or maybe, sarcastically let my Faisalabadi side out, but we did not have that level of frankness between us.

"What I want to tell you is that Gul, my sister, will be staying with us."

"I- I know that." I answered.

"Yes, but you don't know for how long, right?"

"Three weeks?"

"No, she will be staying with us permanently. Now I know that you're a *very,* very, good wife and that you won't have a problem with that. Gul will shift rooms and get the three rooms on the corner for her privacy. We already have massi Kalsoom so you don't have to do anything but I do expect you to give my sister company. She has complained that you don't talk much. No one likes a woman who doesn't talk much. And that you don't respect her interests. If she thinks that some clothes don't suit you, I'm pretty sure that they don't. So don't hurt her feelings and go around buying stuff when she's not around-"

"But *aisi baat nahin hai.* I- I really liked that jumpsuit."

"Let me complete what I'm saying." Nibhaan's tone changed and his face swelled up like Bugs Bunny, the rabbit, without a carrot. He looked funny but instead of laughing, my eyes started tearing up.

"Good wives listen. Look, we're in a different country

and I'm caring about you. We're having fun, aren't we? So when I'm talking, you listen. If you talk and I talk, who listens?"

"Jee."

"My sister Gul has always been different. Before her *shaadi,* she got sick. The doctors didn't know what was wrong with her. Our family doctor who often visited us in the house was a foolish one. He actually blamed her sickness on the house, Sajeer. Doctor *bontar gaya tha.* Anyway, it was nothing contagious. She had fits and saw things. Things that weren't there. *Dewaraein charhti thi.* I felt very sad. *Akhloti bhen meri.* We engaged her to my cousin. Unfortunately, he died in an accident. Tou she married again. This time, however, the man divorced her. Could never love my sister. I know how women work. *Mujhe dekh lo,* of course I'll make you love me. Patience *chahiye hota. Samaj rahi hou na main kya keh raha houn?"*

Samaj tou sab rahi thi. First, Nibhaan had a side to him that I hadn't seen before. He could become a completely different person. Second, Gul and I weren't going to get along because apparently she was a *skaeti-duddo* ¬ and I hadn't even done anything wrong. Third, he just admitted to his sister being mentally ill and he *needed* me to be fine with that. Fourth, I *had* to meet their family doctor. I held the house responsible for a lot of things. Fifth, a whole lifetime of Gul was worse than forced sex with Nibhaan which he thought was mandatory to do each night on the honeymoon.

However, I summed up my thoughts in two words and we left for the beach. "I understand." I said.

The beach was different from Karachi's. The water was saltier because it stung my shaved legs, but it was much cleaner and I spotted no camels peeing nearby. We had booked a private resort and some 'fun' water activities that couples did together – none of which I actually felt like doing. After a satisfying lunch and experiencing drinking juice out of a coconut for the first time, we lay under the sun on borrowed beach mats. I wore my now turned sandy jumpsuit, which I believe made me look slimmer like one of those elite class ladies in Lahore that only eat from Café Aylanto.

My thoughts slowly drifted towards Hashim. I wondered if he was remembering me as much as I remembered him. Do you know how bumblebees make their nests? We had many of those pollinating insects at our colony when *phupho* lived upstairs. They aren't like *shaed ki makhian*. They're hairy, fat and they don't die when they sting. Hashim and I used to call ourselves bumble people. The type who'd sting through *zindagi*. We used to sit in the golden light of April's *dophair*, examining the bees making their nests. They carefully made those tiny pots that appeared to be of clay for tiny people, and then peacefully settled inside. Hashim said that one day, bit by bit, we'd make our own home like the bumblebees. We'd not buy a house, because bought houses are someone else's redecorated dreams and to make a home truly ours, we'd built it.

"What are you thinking about?" Nibhaan whispered in my ear. The sun was setting and the clouds were dressed in purple.

"Nothing." I replied. "The sky looks beautiful."

Nibhaan looked at the sky. "It is very colourful. I wonder how colourblind people appreciate colors."

"Hmm."

"Are you thinking about colour blindness now?"

"Um no," I answered. "I-I'm not thinking about anything. It's good to not think about anything."

"Do you know that bumblebees cannot see the color red?"

I sat up straight and coughed. The coincidence of him mentioning bumblebees was uncanny.

"I did not know that." I replied calmly.

"I think bumblebees are not thankful. They want to live in self-made little houses when they can actually live with a family." Nibhaan replied, shifting his gaze towards me.

I did not answer. I did not know what to say. The sand grains started sticking to my sweaty hands.

"I'm glad we planned this trip. We are getting to know each other. I know you like shrimp. I know you don't like to have sex with me every day. I told you that I like my sister and a good wife who listens to my sister. I'll tell you what I don't like. I don't like liars and bumblebees. I don't mind you thinking about your former love, Sajeer. It's not like you and I will ever leave each other. We're together till our very last breath."

The sky behind Nibhaan turned crimson red.

Chapter

6

The Visitor

When I was young, and one of my eldest cousins wasgetting married, I remember dado telling her something. She said, as I faintly recall, *'Muzammil kahe din hai tou din hai. Muzammil kahe raat hai tou raat hai.'* My little brain couldn't comprehend what it meant at that point, but I often wondered till one day before my *shaadi,* my ama said that very same thing to me whilst braiding my hair. I believe that this phrase is prevalent in *desi* culture. It means that you should by all means agree to what your husband thinks or says. It is one of the basic steps to 'making a cluster of bricks your *ghar'.* But, you see, I saw my dado and dada and they had the bubbliest romance. I saw my ami abu and though no doubt, they omitted toxicity by being slaves to the *'loug kya kahein gay'* mindset, they had been very much in love and not once had ama been petrified of baba and not once had baba let a night pass without sniffing the scent of ama's maroon shawl.

But I could not, no matter how much I pushed myself, agree with Nibhaan. Perhaps, it was because of the Eldritch House or maybe, just maybe I was losing the rationality of my mind. This man, I was forced to call *neebo,* because every time I did so it made him smile, was a rather peculiar being. My period had never been regular and he could guess the day and even the time of its arrival. He knew how long ago I had consumed water and most importantly, he knew when I was thinking about Hashim. He would sniff my arms and tell me that during noon, my body had sipped water from a cup, and then he would after giving it a brief thought, tell me if it was a plastic cup or a metal one. Once, I had Tang from a ceramic cup, and he had licked his plaque-infested teeth, telling me how much art it was to mold glass. This was our 'little game' – smelling the odor of my body and telling me where it had been and what it had done.

The strangest part was, that on Fridays after the *Zohar* prayer, when the *amaam's* sound would echo till the villa, Nibhaan's pale color would turn rosy pink, and his devilish eyes would turn loopy and sleepy and till *Maghrib,* he would be a person I could communicate with. He'd eat, and he'd sit next to me and listen to me, and if I'd say it is night outside, he'd agree to it even if he could see the sunlight pouring in from the glossy window pane.

A month after our *horrormoon,* I started feeling dizzy. It was nothing like I had encountered before. There were huge flashes of light that pinched my eyes, and when I slept, it felt like I was floating across the room. During one such night, I opened my eyes to see that many women with cloaks covering their faces, had lifted me on the top of their heads. They were swinging me in a calm manner, as if I was a baby that they were singing a soothing lullaby to, to help me sleep. During another such night, I slept on the bed and woke up on the floor in the upper corridor. The next day, the entire house started smelling like sweet rice, and sugary *ghee.* Nibhaan was lying next to me and when I opened my eyes, I was greeted by his misshapen grin.

"Sajeer, *meri jaan…"* he said. "Why didn't you tell me before?"

Tell you what? I thought, trying to open my eyes.

"I'm over the moon. So are mama and papa." he continued. *"Bee jaan* told me *subah subah,* just as I was to leave about the news and I thought that I'd stay back and distribute *mithai* all over town."

"Am I pregnant?" I asked. I don't know why I had asked that, but even though I hadn't regained all my senses, I recalled that I had been feeling nauseous and Nibhaan's sudden concern had confirmed the fact.

"What do you mean, *am I.* Of course you are. And I'm *tou naraz jaan.* You should have told me before Gul and *bee jaan."*

"I didn't tell-"

"Chalo utho, shabash. Let's get ready. Mama, papa *saath aj lunch karein gay."*

My head felt heavy and like all other days, none of what was happening made any sense. Anyway, I got up and washed my face. An ironed, floral pink new shirt was neatly hung in my dresser. I did not question how it got there. I felt like a puppet. Nothing in me or around me made sense. I did not know that I was expecting, but everyone else did. Months ago, I would have screamed and run out of the house or probably confronted the made-up lies, but now, I showered calmly. As the lukewarm water trickled down my skin, I tried to remember *when* I had told the others about a pregnancy I myself had no clue about.

We all sat around the dining table. Uncle in his wheelchair, aunty with her heavy bangles, *bee jaan* with her *channa* scent, Gul with her freshly painted nails and Nibhaan with his gleaming, cheerful eyes. This was the first time in months that I had sat next to aunty for enough time to notice her features. I felt as if she had a very forgettable face – as if at the start of the marriage, aunty was a different looking woman. She said little, and carefully separated the potatoes on her plate.

"Carbs…" she said. "They're your enemy."

"But, not yours, my dear." she added. "Your baby needs all the nourishment in the world."

The food was ordered from Hot and Spicy, and even though it happened to be my favorite restaurant, because of my sickness, I felt that everything was too raw to be chewed. My mouth felt teeth-less, and the *boti* was stuck to the roof of it. At the end of the lunch, Gul delightfully announced how being the *phupho*, she'd have to make the major changes in the house. Massi Kalsoom who kept stuffing my plate with meat whispered that the house was ready for a new member, in fact – it was delighted. I scorned and told her to let me be. Nibhaan, seeing my irked attitude, scolded the massi a little more and instructed everyone to take good care of me. The lunch ended with uncle handing me a cheque of a hundred thousand rupees to get all the necessities for myself and the baby.

"But there are still nine months to go." I replied, not trying to sound boorish. "JazakAllah- I mean."

"Itna waqt nahin lage ga." Bee jaan said. I refused to answer her. After seeing her on the plane's wing, I had been frightened for a lifetime. I planned not to argue with her and to make her understand science.

The following morning I requested Nibhaan to drop me at my parents'.

"They're going to be grandparents too!" I exclaimed with forced joy. "I should spend some time with them."

Nibhaan nodded and dropped me to baba's on his way to his work. Over there, before any *salam* or *dua,* I went to the washroom and took out a pregnancy strip wrapped in my *dupatta.* I hadn't taken a pregnancy test before, so I read the instructions thoroughly.

No line meant that the test was invalid. One line meant that it was negative. Two lines meant that it was positive and that I was carrying a chunk of Nibhaan inside me.

I rinsed baba's ashtray, peed in it, put the stick in and nervously waited. As a woman, I had always wanted a baby. I liked the smell of Johnson's baby powder and the taste of Cerelac, and I desired a doll of my own to show the world to. But I did not want Nibhaan's baby. I pulled the stick out. There were two red lines. And then just at that moment, a third one formed. Within a minute, the line had six red lines on it. Horrified, I threw the stick away.

Ama spent the day phoning relatives and baba got me Chaman's ice-cream which was a tradition. Since I had been in school, whenever I did something to please baba, I'd get a scoop of Chaman. I lay down on the sofa bed and watched Titanic on HBO for the seventh time, not because I liked Titanic but because it was always playing on HBO. I wanted to sob, I wanted to get hit by a truck and most importantly I did not want ama to phone *phupho.*

Hours passed, and I stayed at that one position, cursing my flabby stomach. Ama and baba *jee*, left for a *foutgi* to do *afsos* but I secretly knew that ama had persuaded baba to go so that she could *'baatoun baatoun main'* inform everyone about her becoming a *dadi*.

I locked the doors and sat in despair. And then, I started weeping. I wept and wept till the pillow was covered with mucus, drool and salty tears. I then switched its side and wept some more. With tired eyes, I took a nap. The doorbell rang and I sprang up. There was a print of my foundation on ami's cushion. Thinking that my parents had returned, I yelled, *'aai rahi houn'* and then ran to open the door.

My heart skipped a beat and my knees felt wobbly. In front of me stood Hashim with a box of Jalal Son's croissants. His skin was radiant, and he had grown a beard. He looked *better* than he had ever looked.

I smiled sheepishly and said salam. He was more surprised to see me than I was and he did not answer.

"Ama baba *ghar nahin hain.*" I said.

"Oh."

After all that had happened, I expected him to say a little more. Maybe, tell me about his wife-to-be and give an excuse for not inviting me to his big day.

"Andar nahin bulao gi?"

I stepped aside. He handed me the packed box and came in.

"Shaadi ki khushi main?" I inquired.

"No, apke bache ki khushi main."

So ama had told phupho after all. I felt embarrassed. It felt as if I had done something I wasn't supposed to. My flushed cheeks went beetroot red and I wondered if they matched the chum-chums in the mithae box.

"I'm very happy." he said. *"Achi baat hai kay tum*

khsuh hou yaar."

I wanted to hit him. I wanted to pull his gelled back hair and slap him back to his senses. I wanted him to hold me close and tell me that this was all a very bad dream but then, it dawned upon me that he was going to get married and he might have moved on - after all, he had every right to. But, it hurt. My heart hurt. It felt like my board exam result had just come out, as if ama had found out the biggest lie, if someone close to me had died – if *I had died.* Yes, it felt like I had died.

"Tum khush tou hou na?" he said, sensing my silence.

In the books that I had read, the heartbroken woman always said that she was happy. She pretended to be happy. It didn't work any other way. But my story wasn't a book, and if it had to be a book, I didn't want to be *those* women. I wanted to be Sajeer. *Hashim's Sajeer.* And at that very moment, I decided to tell him everything. If it meant to be answered with ignorance and to be shown a picture of his wife.

I sat him down and with tears rolling down my cheeks, I told him *everything.*

At the end of it, Hashim placed his hand on mine. If he could, he would have hugged me, and I felt that with his touch. It wasn't a sorry feeling – it was a touch of longing. Suddenly, out of thin air, something slapped him and Hashim flew to the other side of the room.

Chapter

7

Pakistani Sushi

Two years before my marriage, when Hashim and I were engaged, the entire family went to Murree. I wasn't permitted to sit in Hashim's Suzuki, but each time we stopped at the petrol pump we held hands whilst exchanging Super Crisps. It wasn't lust, it never had been – it was just being very much in love. In fact, years before we had made a pact that we'd not indulge in any *astagfar* activity. Luckily for me, phupho had drunk a lot of Country juice and we needed to stop at every gas station till we reached chacha Abuzar's apartments. With purple-colored jeans, which, by the way, were the only jeans I owned (not because I couldn't buy more, but because I wasn't allowed to wear anything but a *shalwar,* and an oversized *kurti),* I trekked between the mountains with Hashim. The route had already been made safe but we pretended that we were on a risky mission with a limited amount of Cadbury Perks, and for survival we had to collect stones. Later on, we got tired and started walking under the clear blue sky. I liked how Hashim was a child at heart, so transparent and committed. We spotted houses and decided that one day when he'd have earned enough, we'd come and settle between the mountains like dado's sister. He'd paint and I'd garden. It seemed so doable and simple back then. How could we not make promises with *thaandi hawein* running between the strands of our hair, the *badal-less asmaan* knitting clouds out of the words we uttered, and spiritual hugs from the chalky mud that dripped from our toes?

I patted the cold towel on Hashim's cheek.

"Did it hurt?"

"Did what hurt?"

"The *thappar* yaar," I answered and drenched the towel.

"It hurts knowing that I've spent so many months thinking of you and telling myself that I'll never have you." he replied. "But, that's the thing about loving someone, you always have hope."

I smiled. "I know."

We sat, holding hands with our backs leaning against the sofa bed. Hashim clenched my palm. *"Jitne thapar marne hai mar lo,* I'm not leaving her hand."

I laughed. *"Ahista bolo. Ama jee na sun lain."*

I felt as one feels after finally breathing through a blocked nose; happy.

"So, what do you think? Is it the haunted house or is my husband a jinn or something?"

Hashim sighed. "I don't believe that jinns are bad,

you know. They're good folks and they don't really hurt people. *Theek hai, gusah aya, thapar mar diya.* If you were mine, I would *tou* have stabbed the person with mammy's *churi* you know."

We didn't know what to talk about. I had told him about the villa and its inhabitants and he had shown me a picture of his fiancé. If we could, at that very moment we would have run away. The old us would have started investigating the paranormal experience that had just occurred with Hashim, but our mature reaction surprised me. I wasn't frightened and neither was he.

"I do not want you to suffer." Hashim said.

"The moment you let go, the suffering will start." I commented.

Hashim pecked my forehead. "It'll all be fine, Sajeer. *Likun,* for now, we need to think about how you can get out of this mess. *Pata hai,* I know this way of doing *ruqya,* it's a soul cleansing method. *Itna koyi mushqhil nahin hai.* All you need to do is memorize some verses and recite them around the people of the house. No one will bother you."

"*Main tou namaz bhi nahin parhti.*"

"That isn't a problem. Do you want me to write the verses down? Come on, let me help you."

"Why do you know them by heart?" I interrogated playfully. "If these sonnets of yours solved issues, I would have been your wife *ab tak.*"

I placed my head on his lap and looked at his uneven beard. He was beautiful. He was someone God would make on a Sunday afternoon. And I knew that he had been gift-wrapped and sent for me. How could my heart be away from a piece of itself for long? I was just being tested, of that I was sure.

Hashim folded my cuffs and scribbled some Arabic

on my arms. I did not want him to stop. I wanted him to cover my entire body with ink. *I wanted him to ink his name on me.*

"I have to go now." he said after handing me the ballpoint. "I won't marry her, *wesay.*"

"Stay a bit longer." I insisted. "Please."

"Mammu mammy ki awazein aa rahi hain. I should go."

I nodded and let go of his hand. He then pressed his cold cheek against my cracked foundation.

"Kam make-up kiya karo." he joked.

He stood next to me for a bit and then left through the back door. As soon as he left, ama entered the lounge. She was accompanied by baba and a bag full of groceries. The jar of Olive Groove butter spread could be seen through the thin plastic bag hanging from her wrist.

I took a huge breath and began to help her assemble the items on the ground. *"Afsos karne gaein thien ap tou."*

"Haan socha groceries bhi pakar loun."

"Why wasn't the door locked. *Koyi aya tha kya?"*

I paused for a second and bit my lip. *"Phupho ki taraf say mithae ayi thi."*

I then pointed towards the Jalal Son's box on the kitchen shelf. *"Kha lain."*

Ama looked at me and raised her eyebrows. "That box has *phewian* and your baba brought it in the morning. Phupho isn't even home."

Rather than fetching the box and showing her that it did indeed have sweets in it, I stopped talking. Eventually, she would have asked who dropped it by and I would have had to tell her about Hashim.

"I'm going to go sleep." I said. *"Koyi kaam tou nahin hai?"*

"Go wash your face and put on my mascara. Nibhaan is coming to pick you up."

"Jee?"

"Haan jee."

I told ama that I had come for some days and that I wasn't leaving the house, especially now that I knew that Hashim and I were to meet again the next day. But Nibhaan had already called baba and asked if he could come to pick me. It was because of yet another family dinner. Over the months, we never had any dinners and now suddenly the disoriented *khandaan* of his wanted to reunite over food and the *khushi* of a child I did not want.

Blackmailing ama emotionally about how much I missed her did not work. She fixed me up like one of those rag dolls from my *bachpan* by powdering my face with cosmetics and sent me back home. In all honesty, I was very close to starching Nibhaan's face during the car ride, but like a lifeless *kapray ki guria,* I stayed quiet. Today I had been blessed with Hashim's touch and to me that had been enough. When I was young and had lots of algebraic questions to solve, I sipped milo before each one, thinking that it would help me get through that one question. And, just like that, Hashim's presence had given me enough calmness to get through the night.

When I reached home, everyone was waiting by the door. I learned that we were going out for seafood, because I, the *dulhaan* of the house loved it, and so on Nibhaan's demand, everyone had gotten dressed to please me and spend the night as a family. I pictured Hashim and smelled my hand. My face twinkled. Nothing else mattered anymore.

We arrived at Sumo, a small and homely place situated next to Hardees. Uncle *jee* was carried upstairs by Nibhaan and aunty hid her face as if it was an embarrassing thing to do. Gul was dressed as if it were her *shaadi,* and I felt sorry for her. *Bee jaan* had actually brought a tiffin of *channay* along. I felt like we were the Addams Family. Nibhaan had reserved a table under my name and I sensed that did not sit well with Gul. Everyone except me ordered fish. I feasted on a vibrant sushi platter.

"You seem different." Gul said with her mouth full of churned fish.

I felt different. I felt invincible.

"I don't like it." Gul added. "*Kuch tou garbar hai.*"

Gul was a pest. I had not been able to comprehend her doings and I knew for a fact that she was going to speak about my 'changed *bartao*' to her brother. Whilst we waited for the bill, I slid up my sleeve and took a good look at what Hashim had penned down. I started to mumble the verses. It was hard to say the words in a flow, which had never been the case during my Quran recitations. It seemed as if the letters weren't from the holy book. But of course, I didn't think much about it. Hashim had given them, and he was the only *namazi* I knew after baba.

My jaw would lock completely on the fourth word and I had to practice under my breath a couple of times before I could say it but *I wanted to say it.* It felt powerful – like some sort of energy moving through my veins. But of course, as Hashim had informed, it was to ward off evil and there was nothing more sinister than Gul sitting across me with her glittering, nosy existence. I looked at her and started to mumble the verses repeatedly. Nothing happened.

I thought that she would react because possessed people react, at least that is what I had read in horror books and seen in Vikraal and Gubraal. I looked at *Bee jaan* and started again. I stopped midway because her glare was discomfiting. It felt that she was looking right through my soul. Something about what I was doing was intimidating and I did not want to back down so I shifted my glance towards my *nand* and started to repeat the act.

The fork that Gul was playing with slipped from her hand and she froze. I panicked and closed my mouth but inside, my tongue kept on moving. It was as if it was on its own. The waiter approached the table with a fill-me card and just then, Gul started to bang her head on the table. Everyone started staring at us. Nibhaan placed his hand on the table so that Gul would not hurt herself and *Bee jaan* quickly turned on the Quran application from her flashy Q-mobile. During the entire time, I could not stop quoting the Arabic under my breath. Aunty and a couple of waiters started to pin Gul to the carpeted children's area near our table. Stunned by what I was seeing, I felt my hands nervously shake. I attempted to bite my tongue but in vain. Gul started to rise above the floor despite five men trying to hold her down. She levitated till the height of our table in front of everyone and then fell to the ground. My tongue stopped moving.

Chapter

8

New Beginnings

It was difficult to sleep at night with the hurling screams and groaning voices coming from across the door. The atmosphere in the corridor was freezing cold, and other than Nibhaan no one dared step inside Gul's room. It had been four weeks since the sushi incident, and Gul's condition had only worsened. She couldn't sleep unless she was sedated and when awake, she'd refer to herself as 'Anjali' and speak in a language we couldn't comprehend. In the morning, the doctors would treat her and at night, *bee jaan* would bring a molvi from the mosque. According to the doctors, she had dissociative identity disorder and because of that, she had assumed herself to be an Indian goddess. But the karih sahib said that '*saaya hou gaya hai'* and later on when an elderly *bazurg* from Nibhaan's office stepped in, we were informed that Gul had in fact been possessed by multiple Hindu jinns, all above the age of two hundred. Upon more investigation into the matter, we later found out that the language she spoke was ancient Sanskrit and that a special *'phonchay huwe'* sahib had to be called in for her treatment.

I felt that I had very little to contribute to the situation. What had happened at the restaurant had been a coincidence. Mere words could not have such a powerful and devilish effect. Plus, these demonic entities know everything and if I had been responsible for Gul's sickness, they probably would have blurted it out. A week before the *phonchay huwe sahib* had to arrive, I made alphabet soup for Gul. It was just *yakhni* with edible packet alphabets. She had mentioned that it was something she had in Dubai. Instead of being thankful, she hissed and poured the hot soup over me. I screamed in agony. Nibhaan quickly took me away and layered my lap with mycitracin. During the entire process, Nibhaan's facial expressions changed and at that point in time, I figured out that his personality had altered. It was an everyday thing that happened during spccific hours starting from *zuhar* time. There was this calm Nibhaan that showed affection and listened to me with attention. His face was full of *noor,* and he was relaxed with not the slightest worry in life. Then, there was the Nibhaan whose nostrils expanded, who sniffed me from head to toe and could read my mind and at that very moment, it was the latter Nibhaan that I was dealing with.

Nibhaan's soft touch turned into a harsh one and he started aggressively rubbing the cream on my belly.

"You're – you're hurting me." I said and tried to pull away. "Stop it, Nibhaan."

But he kept at it – and my skin started to develop a rash. I started kicking my legs in the air and tugging his arm. "Stop it. Stop it! It's making the pain worse!"

Nibhaan stopped and suddenly jumped on top of me.

"The door is open!" I responded, with warm tears rolling down my cheeks.

"I'm not going to *fuck* you." a reply came. "Not when you've been stained with your lover's hands. But you see, the joke is on you, you *slut.*"

With my eyes wide open and a burning stomach, I slowly started to move from under him.

"Please – please let me go."

Nibhaan grabbed me by the hair and pulled me back up.

"Hear me and hear me well. I have tried to love you. I have tried but a woman like you can never be loyal. Do you think that you can go back home and deceive me? I will rob you of your senses. *You never* did go home. You never left the premises. The house didn't let you. You sat in the living room and talked to your mama and in that very living room you sat and held my hand and called me Hashim."

I started to tremble. "No – no, you're lying. I was home. I held Hashim's hand."

Nibhaan pressed his sweaty hands on my chest and dug my nails into my skin. I felt like ama's rosy green *dupatta* that had been caught between the thorns which she had just rigorously pulled apart.

"I'm sorry." I begged. "P-please."

"Call your mama. And ask her. I want to see your face when you realize."

His hot breath stung my forehead. "Call her."

I reached for my phone and called ama.

Dil main meray hai darde-bhutto, darde-bhutto. Iss

tune ko apni ringtone bnane kay liye abhi hash ka button dubaein. Siraf panch rupay das paisa..

"Haan Sajeer beta, kya haal hai." Baba picked up.

Nibhaan glared at me. "Baba," I said with all the energy I could, *"Main theek houn.* Can I talk to ama?"

Baba handed the phone to ama. "Sajeer *ka phone hai."*

"Ama, *baat sunain meri gour say,* the moment I got pregnant, *us din* did I come to your house right?"

"Na koyi salam, na koyi dua, is this what I've taught you, hain?"

"Ama please, just answer me."

I felt like I would collapse at any given moment but I had to keep on going because there was a monstrous ogre breathing down my neck.

"What did you ask?" ama inquired carelessly. "I'm near the washing machine *tou* the voice is breaking."

"Tell me if this happened. Did I or did I not come home to tell you about my pregnancy? And then when I did, you had gone to chacha Abuzar's foutgi for afsos. You came back with a bag of groceries. I wanted to stay-"

"Beta, what nonsense. Your chacha is very much alive."

"Amiii, please! Just listen. I came and then I wanted to stay but then Nibhaan called baba for permission and we went to a sushi restaurant."

"Okay, *main kya bolun?"*

My throat was getting dry and Nibhaan dug his nails a little more into the wounded area. I shrieked in pain.

"Is this one of your jokes *beta?* You did not come. It's been more than a month. *Maine aur apke baba nay ana hai with mithae* and lots of gifts for our nawasa to be. Your baba says that he's sure it's a b-"

I cut the call and started to weep hysterically. "I don't know what's happening. I don't know why ama is lying.

She is busy shaid-"

"Your mama isn't lying." Nibhaan gritted. "You *never* left the house. The house gives you what you want. It shows you that. And the fact that you don't want your husband is as disgusting as it gets!"

Nibhaan pushed me away and I tumbled off the bed. I lay on the floor drinking salty tears as he walked out of the room and shut the door behind him. The marble felt nice next to my burnt skin.

Years ago, I collected coins from my house and spent them on a gum called Bubble Your Name. I really thought that one day, the gum would spell my name. Days went by and I found a gum with Hashim's name on it. The m was a little incomplete and Hashim said that it spelled H-a-s-h-i-r, but I told him that Hashir was no name. We, later on, said that it was Allah's way of telling us that we belonged together. After the ring ceremony on our engagement, I narrated this very incident to Hashim and he said that he couldn't for the life of it remember when I had been fond of gums and had found his name on one. When I persisted, he pretended to recall it.

Whatever was happening was making me believe that there was something wrong with me – my head and my sanity. Gul didn't need the treatment, I did. *I needed to be cured of this altered reality.*

Khair, after getting hiccups and chewing on my misery, I had a bath and got my burns treated with *bee jaan's* herbal *kooti huwi* medicine. She said nothing whilst tenderly applying the paste to my skin and wrapping me in a towel. She didn't even ask how I had gotten hurt but rather offered me to nibble on some *channay* which she believed to have majestic healing abilities. And I did. I gobbled up all her steamed chickpeas. For the first time, I saw *bee jaan* smile a smile of contentment.

Days passed and I started to lose sense of it all. There were times when I saw Gul standing in the kitchen whereas she was locked in her room the whole time. Even though she was the one who urinated on the stairs and pointed towards her vagina whilst running naked in the corridor, I thought I was the one who was demented. Her deteriorating health had made her the size of a *gootli-less aam,* and at night, with her eyes turned upwards, she was often seen sitting on top of the doors, humming to herself. I had the terrible gut feeling that somehow, I would end up like Gul.

There is little time between a piece of corn popping into a popcorn and then turning roasted black if the heat is not turned off. I felt that I had reached that point of exhaustion and that there was little life left in me: everything was going black. But, during this time, I often found myself pondering about Hashim. I believed that in all this chaos, he would be the only one to make sense of it. I thought that if I cannot get to him during my stay in this house, I somehow have to get out of the villa. And the only key to getting out was my kooky, sorry excuse for a husband.

I waited for when Nibhaan's bushy face shone and his upright figure knelt down. I waited for when in his bloodshot eyes appeared some empathy. And when the time came, I wore my best dress and sat next to him. He looked at me in a pleasant manner.

"You look pretty today, Mash Allah. The child is adding so much glow to your face!" he remarked.

"Thank you, *neebo.* If you're not too occupied, can we talk?"

"Even if I were occupied, I would have made time for you my *jaan.*"

I sat him down and held his hand. I told him that

the boredom was getting to my head. I mentioned how it is important for the child's well-being that I have happy thoughts. The point where he started looking concerned, I told him what I wanted.

I placed his hand on my stomach and told him to agree for the sake of our child.

"Btao bhi jaan, what is that you want? *Jo hukam ho apka."*

"Kinnaird College for women is offering these lifetime learning courses. They're for a couple of weeks and I'm not even showing yet. I- I want to get enrolled in one of those. Morning shift-"

"That's perfectly fine, *likun* have you thought of a course and are you doing it because you want to or is there some sort of pressure from aunty? If you want to get out of the house, we can go to the Northern areas. Massi Kalsoom and the new helpers will look after Gul."

The last thing I wanted was to be *alone* with him and his mercurial, oscillating, split personality.

I shook my head. "No, no," I replied. "Gul is ill and she needs all your attention. I can bring the laptop over right now. I can make the payment and get enrolled-"

"Haan haan, wou sab tou theek hai baby, but what is the course?"

"Psychology. Or even Literature. I haven't thought it through. You know how I've always been inclined towards both. So what do you think?"

Nibhaan looked at me. "Hmmm, okay." he agreed after some silence. *"Bus ap khush raho."*

I gulped and felt my body at ease. I was going to be away every day for the rest of the month till I could find a way to contact Hashim and get out of this mess, even if it meant never being able to meet baba again.

Chapter

9

Bun in the Oven

The building of Kinnaird College wasn't foreign to me. Before going to BNU, I had done my intermediate from Kinnaird. The corridors greeted me with a warm breeze every day. I'd get dropped hours before the lecture and long after it I'd stay to have some delectable white sauce pasta served in paper plates with a sachet of dried oregano. Mariam, a former friend from FSC who now handled the bio lab, told me that the secret to the pungent aftertaste was Rahim – the canteen *wala's paseena*. She believed that it dripped from his face into the sizzling hot oil the pasta was being prepared in and added the flavor. Mariam was hilarious. I was glad that someone from before was around – made me feel at peace.

I had always been bad at keeping secrets. I told people that I was a great secret keeper and that only when I fought with the person would I become a telltale but, the truth was that at one point in life, I had thrived on gossip. Don't mistake me for one of those mean girls with hair ironed from Deepilex daily and who can't eat fries because 'ew oil'. *But,* I had no *deen eman* when it came to keeping things to myself. I was the type who'd gather the news, spice it up with some *chaat masala,* and share it among my friends. So now, when I had been so oblivious to the world's happenings, Mariam questioned how much I had changed. And just then, with white sauce sticking to my fingers, I told her my tale.

"Wow," she replied. "I always thought you'd end up with Hashim, you know. This is awful *yaar.*"

"I *will* end up with Hashim." I said. *"Dekh lena."*

"Acha thora pasta tou dou."

Mariam wasn't interested in what was happening to me. But girl friendships are like that. We pretend to be friends but deep down, we don't really care. It's just for time-pass and birthday surprises. But, still. I was glad to have a familiar face around even if it meant paying for that face's wheat treat each day.

Mariam stuffed her mouth and gave me a pat on the back. *"Dekho,"* she said whilst munching. "You're married now. Maybe, *just* maybe if you try to love Nibhaan things will work out."

I couldn't stop thinking about how oddly shaped Mariam's body was. She wasn't fat, she wasn't slim and she certainly wasn't chubby either. Her breasts were the wildest I had seen – either that or she wore no bra. Instead of being plump and straight, they were sagging and going sideways – *jasie aik doosre say naraz houn.* And she had even named them. One was Rajesh and the other was Kumar. I shrugged.

"We can't just *try* to love." I answered. "It happens naturally. Yes, I can get attached to Nibhaan but I can't love him, because my heart beats for Hashim and recognizes him, and if I know what love is, it is because of Hashim."

Mariam rolled her eyes. "You and your philosophies."

"You'd know when you fall in love, Mariam."

"Bhai," she said, eyeing my coke. *"Meri suno tou* snap out of this Hashim phase. He's getting married too. *Har din hum yahan beth kay usi ki baat karte hain.* And somehow, I think it doesn't matter. He doesn't matter."

Mariam's opinion didn't matter. She didn't know what a nutcase my husband was. She didn't know how conservative my parents were. And most importantly, she didn't know what *love* was.

Eventually, in between the Literature course that I had taken, Mariam stopped hanging out with me. Her father was a religious man and when she had shared the happenings in my house with him, he had strictly forbidden her to see me.

"Us kay saath saaye mandrate hain. Wou tumhari shaadi main rukawat bune gi."

The only *'rukawat'* in Mariam's *shaadi* would have been her parting breasts.

So one of those days when I was sitting by myself and having pasta, I thought that it was best to contact Hashim. Years back when I was an inter-student, we'd end up in the McDonald's near my college, share a one fifty rupee burger and giggle away our little worries. Those were the best days of my life. And so, I stood right outside that McDonald's and phoned him.

My fingers went key to key, and I dialed his number without even looking at my mobile.

"Hello?"

"Salam Sajeer, um, kesi ho?"

Little chum-chums danced in my belly.

"Hello? Sajeer?"

I gulped. "Haan, I'm here. *Kaisay ho* Hashim?"

"Main fit faaat. Shaadi ki tyaarion main masroof."

"Oh."

"I'm sorry. That was insensitive of me. I shouldn't have said that." he replied. "You tell. *Kaisay yaad karna huwa?"*

I had known Hashim all my life. He was jealous and he wanted me to pay for it. I knew it.

Two can play this game.

"Acha, can we meet?" I said. "We can discuss everything then. I want to see you."

"Mammy *jaan kay ghar ayi huwi ho?"*

"No, I'm at McDonald's – jail road *wala*. You know, our spot. When can you come?"

"Just the two of us? Won't that be awkward? *Yah Nibhaan bhai aa rahe hain?"*

I closed my eyes. Hashim and his jealousy. But I couldn't let him get the better of me.

"Acha na, I am sorry. What do you want me to say, that I love you? Of course, you know that already. *Aaa tou jao. Sab pareshanian dour kardoun gi."*

"Tumhari tabiyat theek nahin lag rahi mujhe, Sajeer."

"Are you coming or not?" I scoffed. "I'm waiting."

"Of course I'm not coming. *Bhen,* next week *meri shaadi hai.* Don't call me again."

I stared at my phone. Hashim hung up. I felt my heart sink. The weather was humid and yet, I felt shivers run down my spine. He was playing hard to get, he had to be. Or worse – Nibhaan must have done something. What if – What if he was making Hashim say all those things against his will?

I called Hashim again and he disconnected the call. I sent him a few question marks via text. After some time, I was blocked from every social media platform. I couldn't zoom in and see his display photo at Bhera. I quietly sat in my car and went home.

The next few days were very difficult. I had lost my appetite and I refused to go to college. I stayed in my room and just got up when Nibhaan came. He tried asking me what was wrong and I said that it was a failed test, but in all honesty, it was failed love. My body had gone numb. *Bee jaan* insisted on a *'sar ki malish'* and even though I didn't want any, the woman had been nice to me earlier so I agreed. The following week for each day, I sat between her emaciated legs, and got my hair oiled with a terrible smelling homemade treatment.

Among all things that were hard to believe, this was different, it came as no surprise in the *bhoot bangla* that I was living in: Within seven days, my thin hair which fell till my shoulders grew till my knees and became thick as the threads in ama's shawl. Two months had passed since I had first found out about my pregnancy and yet, my stomach had expanded so much that I looked and felt like a nine-month pregnant woman. I could not recognize myself in the mirror.

The *'phonchay huwe baba'* gave up hope on Gul. He said that the jinns had infested every part of her body and even if he could banish them, Gul's memory had forever been impaired. Aunty and uncle signed the papers and got Gul admitted to a psychiatric facility in Islamabad. When Gul was being led out of the house, each time she looked at my stomach, the child inside me kicked. Astonished, I quickly turned around and went to my room.

"Nibhaan," I said, one day after *zuhar.* "I should see a doctor. I don't feel so well and look at my size. I don't think it's normal for a two-month-old child."

Nibhaan put down the newspaper and stared at me. "Every woman's body is different, *jaan*. Doctors just ruin things. Look at what they did to Gul."

"But Gul wasn't pregnant. I am."

"Tell you what," Nibhaan replied. "I am going to Germany for a few weeks. I wanted it to be a surprise but *chalo*. It's for a merger with a company. I will take you along too. You can explore Berlin and I'll do work. It'll be great for the baby and you."

The last time I had traveled alone with Nibhaan, I had suffered. But, I *did* need a change. Thinking about how hurtful Hashim had been, I agreed to the plan.

I was later told that even during the end of days, I wasn't to see a doctor. *Bee jaan* had delivered quite a few babies in the family and she was to deliver mine in a hot tub. But since this was seven months away, I decided to not argue but no way was I going to let *bee jaan* deliver the child. Don't get me wrong, I cared for my safety, not Nibhaan's child's with whom, by the way, I hadn't developed any bond.

A day before our flight, I had the eeriest experience. It was difficult for me to bathe because I couldn't bend and I couldn't see my toes so I sat in an old Shark themed swimming pool that aunty had gotten from Liberty gol *chakar,* years ago. Nibhaan had fixed the holes with some duct tape. Massi Kalsoom fed me chilled mangoes and *meethay parhattaay* as I lay in the water till wrinkles formed on my skin.

So the day before, I had been utterly busy packing new jumpsuits that I had gotten, and by the time I was ready to soak my body in water, it was almost Maghrib time. I came from a family where women were instructed to shut their doors and roll up their windows during

Maghrib. We were told to tie our hair and not wear any perfume. All because *shayateen* came out during that time. I failed to understand why the jinns only attacked women in Pakistan. So, I put on my kurti and went and sat in the partially filled pool.

Silence surrounded me and the only buzzing that could be heard was of the mosquitoes. Moments later, I heard a faint cry. It sounded like someone was calling out to their ami.

Mama.

Ma. Ma.

Mama.

It was a distant cry but somehow it seemed as if the source was nearby. It continued for another minute and during that time I figured out that it was a child calling out and he or she was nearby and was deliberately whispering.

"The voice is probably being blocked by the bush-covered walls. *Saath wale ghar ka bacha rou raha hou ga,*" I assured myself and started creating ripples in the cold water.

Mama.

I sat up and looked around.

Mama. Ma Ma.

No one was anywhere near and the wall was far away. The voice was getting clearer and it was *very very* near. I couldn't look ahead because my gigantic, unwaxed stomach was blocking my view. I stood up and took a bird's eye view of the garden. There was no one in sight.

I sat back down.

Mama. Mama.

A soft child's voice.

I placed my head on my stomach and decided to take a little nap.

Mama.

I jumped in fright. The mama I had just heard had come from inside my stomach. I hadn't been a student of science but as far as I knew, two-month-old children didn't speak. In fact, nine-month-old children didn't speak. No child in the mother's womb spoke.

I placed my head close to my tummy again.

Mama. Mama.

It was my child.

I took a deep breath and placed my ear on my stomach. *I had to be sure.*

Mama. A baby's cry.

Mama. Mama. A baby's voice.

MAMA. A strong, manly shriek. MAMA!

I lost consciousness.

Chapter

10

The End

The frosty crisp wind tapped me on the shoulder and woke me up. I was still lying in the pool. I splashed some water on my face and got up to turn off the pipe. The pool was full and the night was young. I hadn't been unconscious for long because the clatter of the dishes could be heard from the kitchen – which meant that Massi Kalsoom had just served dinner to uncle. My body felt weak and even though the weather was briskly cold, I wanted to spend a few more minutes in it to gather my thoughts. I couldn't for the life of me recall what had happened.

My thinking was disrupted by the sound of the jeep's honking outside. Nibhaan had returned. I got up and rolled my wet hair into a rough bun. Before I could reach for the towel, I felt a scaly movement up my legs. It felt as if the rough, back surface of a foot massager was toggling between my thighs. I only thing I could see was my stomach so I let it go, thinking that it could be my *kurti's* tassel. But, the moment I started walking, it felt like a cold, *cold,* thing had been thrust up the vaginal canal. Petrified, I bent a little and placed my hand from behind my buttocks to pull whatever was dangling there. With a few guessed aims, my fingers wrapped themselves around a moist, flaky exterior which was constantly in motion. I quickly pulled it towards the ground. At first, it didn't nudge, but then I tried harder which led to a tight, cramp in my vagina. Moaning, I pulled the fleshy entity with all my might and when I felt that nothing but air rubbed against my clitoris, I stopped pulling. A splash of liquid appeared on the ground and I bounced backward. There, lying in front of me, covered in a sticky liquid was a baby snake-like creature. It started wriggling towards me. Mama.

I yelled at the top of my voice and dashed back inside.

* * *

"So you're saying that a snake came out of your vagina?" the doctor asked with a raised eyebrow. "And it was stuck, and you pulled it?"

I nodded. "I've gone over it so many times."

"Yes, but I've examined your canal. There was no rash, sign of infection or even bacteria that would have been if a snake was nested-"

"Nibhaan *ap hi baat karlain,*" I replied.

Nibhaan looked at both the doctor and I and sighed. He then signaled the doctor to follow him outside and

200

closed the door behind me.

All the guards and even aunty had done a scavenger hunt for the reptile in the garden but nothing had been found. When I hadn't stopped weeping, a doctor had been called to take a look. The baby was fine, and according to the doctor, was two months old and the enlargement of the womb was because of a condition that I needed not worry about. And of course, he insisted on me taking a nap because the stress had caused me to imagine a snake.

But a baby serpent had slithered out of me and of that I was sure.

Nibhaan bathed me with the help of massi Kalsoom and caressed my body with Johnson's baby powder before dressing me up for the flight. I couldn't help but wonder why he was being *nice* to me. Nibhaan wasn't nice in my head.

The flight to Germany was exhausting. We landed in Munich, which was a breathtaking place and shortly left for Berlin. Nibhaan even insisted that I stand near the marshy woodlands so that he could photograph me. "We'll show these to the baby," he said. I had Starbucks for the first time in my life and unlike what I had seen all my life, my name on coffee cup was spelled correctly. I was beginning to temporarily enjoy life.

Every day Nibhaan would leave for his conferences and office work and give me some euros to spend on food and travel. He permitted me to do anything and everything. I thought that the sun would set and I would see the horrid Nibhaan again but it did not happen. I guess the German winds did it for us. And as important as other details are, I also got my first orgasm in a not so shabby, breakfast in bed serving motel. But of course, I had gotten it thinking of Hashim.

My world changed during our last week in Berlin.

I had just come back from a museum tour, which if I might mention – was a complete rip-off. I paid a hefty amount to see sculptures cut in half from the eighteenth century and if you ever visit baba's house, you can see such headless sculptures dumped in the garage that ama and Bano tayi bought from Anarkali in 2008. Anyway, with a Starbucks smoothie in my hand, I went back to my room. I found the door to be unlocked which was unusual. I knocked it open and stepped inside. Nibhaan was sitting with his face dumped in the pillow, clearly distressed.

"Salam. I'm back."

Nibhaan did not answer me.

"What's wrong?" I asked, placing my drink on the television stand. "Did the meeting not go well?"

Nibhaan sat up and instructed me to close the door.

"I have phoned *your* mama," he replied. "And *your* papa. So whatever follows, they are aware of it."

I came and nestled myself close to him. For the first time, I did not want him to be upset. I was appreciating the lifestyle and if I wanted more of it, it meant I had to have more of Nibhaan.

"*Haan,* but what's wrong?" I questioned nervously.

"Mama had a heart attack earlier today. The doctors couldn't figure out what was the issue-"

"Oh my god. Aunty was in such good health-"

"No. Stop talking," Nibhaan cut in at once, "I will do the talking today. You will just sit and listen. Not another word from you."

He was too tired to be angry but I could sense the stress in his voice.

"Mama's heart gave up and she was the liveliest soul I knew. Before being loaded into the ambulance on the stretcher, she took your name. She told *bee jaan* that she saw you in the house and you.."

Nibhaan's voice trailed off.

"That's not true *na jaan,*" I replied, "I'm *tou* here, with you."

"I told you not to talk. Don't."

Nibhaan grabbed my drink and placed it in my hands. "Drink this. Don't talk."

I stared at my purple lip print on the straw and then at him. We had been told in school that people react differently to sorrow and shocks and it is only natural to answer them as they want to be answered. If Nibhaan wanted to me to stop talking, I had to *stop talking*.

"My mama died an hour ago. The business deal – the biggest of my entire career, was signed off because of unfortunate events. My sister is in a psychiatric hospital. And this is all because of you."

I stopped sipping my smoothie. It was as if the crushed berries had turned sour.

I wanted him to deal with his sorrow, but not put the blame on me. I opened my mouth but Nibhaan put his finger on my lips.

"I saw you at a friend's wedding. I liked you, I really did. I liked the way your nose twitched before you laughed, I liked how you always *tried* to make gol *rottis,* I liked how you call 'ray', 'rray' in Urdu like a typical Lahori, I liked it so much. So mama and papa approached your parents. Your *baba* agreed *forun* but your mama needed time to think. It wasn't because you were engaged to your cousin, it was because of something else. So one day, Sajeer, she came to my house to talk to me. She told me what marrying you meant. She said that in their family, girls had been married to jinns. I thought that it was a joke but her facial expressions told another story. Your dado's sister wasn't the last woman to be approached by a jinn.

When she had been approached by one, her mama had disapproved and so the jinn had gone. This – whatever this is- happens because of a debt that your ancestors took from the jinns, and it won't stop. So, one day your mama started to dream about a jinn asking for your hand in marriage. It was when you were a child. Your mama didn't permit it to see you, but then when the jinn showered your baba with opportunities, your mama with a house and jewels that shone from rooms away, you mama *agreed.* She said yes, Sajeer. She told the jinn that *yes,* my daughter is *rightfully yours.* No one's, but yours. Then, when you became of age, the jinn came to take you away and you mama did everything she could to keep the jinn away. She broke her promise, and she approached all sorts of people to help you heal. You mama broke her pact with a jinn. And then, the jinn started doing *'hazri',* on your cousin Hashim. This sinister thing, possessed him for years so that fire and clay could unite. When your phupho found out, she took Hashim away and got powerful *ruqya* done. During this time, my *rishta* came and you were told that Hashim wasn't good for you and that he wasn't stable, but the truth was that leaving you was the only option he had to become stable. Your phupho met me, and told me that his son never remembered loving you, in fact, most of his memory had been manipulated. I didn't believe all this hocus pocus. My mama baba had given me all the luxuries of life, and when I wanted you, they *had* to give me you. I loved you. From the very first day. Then, I fell ill. I didn't have flu or a treatable cough. My body would be inhabited by an entity and I could not pray, I could not blink without its permission. I knew the jinn had come. *But,* I still loved you for the nights when the jinn wasn't there. Hashim, your cousin came to our marriage but you didn't recognize him, because in your mind, you had seen your jinn's face and now that Hashim had healed, he looked nothing like it. You used to call me Hashim, and I didn't mind. I never hurt you – it was the jinn, who hurt you. It hurt you for wanting me, for being with me, and all this time you thought that I hurt you. I could never. I loved you. The jinn would appear in front of mama, and because of me, she started staying out. She wanted us to work. *Bee jaan* spent months trying to cure you, and Gul? My poor sister was bossy, no doubt but she had lost her husband, and despite that, she was so happy for me. For us. And look at what your jinn did to her. Her brain has forgotten how to chew food. I didn't stop loving you. I loved you with even more force. I saw the jinn make love to you at nights, hurt you till you wept and I took you in my arms and consoled you. I know that this child is not mine. I know that because before yesterday night, I never in my right mind slept with you. But I accepted it. For us. And when you said that a snake wriggled out of you, I believed you and contacted aunty. I was instructed to fly you seas apart because the jinn couldn't follow us and I did. I thought of us moving here. Every day. And look at what happened back home. I realized that no matter what happens – even if I take you away from the jinn – your mind will always love it."

I didn't know what to say. I wanted to say something at that moment. But nothing came out. For the first time in life, I could explain that I was not mentally sick. Now, when Nibhaan wanted me to speak, I *did not know what to tell him.*

"I am sorry for this," Nibhaan continued. "But, *main, Nibhaan, apne poore hosh hawas main, Sajeer, aapko talaq deta haoun. Talaq deta houn…*"

"S-stop," I said. A tear rolled down my cheek. "So, I am well. Nothing is wrong with me. And Hashim isn't even my cousin – Hashim – the jinn – Hashim, is real?"

Nibhaan shut his eyes and took a deep breath. "I thought that you stopped me because you had hope for us."

"I-"

"Do you?"

Hashim was real and he was jealous. I knew my Hashim. He couldn't really hurt me. He was doing this because I was hurting *him.* I was his to begin with.

I saw Nibhaan's eyes water up.

"Tumhe talaq deta houn."

An unexpectedly chilly wind came from the window. It was a calling that I had felt before – at my house, at phupho's house, at Jail road McDonald's, at the trekking park in Murree. I quickly ran towards the window. Out the window, between the road and rushing cars, stood Hashim – with his arms wide open waiting for me to run into them. *I was home.*

About the Author

Ayesha Muzaffar is a nationwide bestselling author who writes tales about the unseen. She is best known for her paranormal short stories that deeply explore the beliefs rooted in the South Asian culture. She lives in Lahore with her husband and a ghost child which her husband claims to never have seen.

Also by Ayesha Muzaffar

If there's something Pakistanis love more than December shaadis and desi food, it`s jinn stories. Jinnistan is a gripping collection of South Asian short horrors featuring paranormal entities in all shapes and forms-including the form of a loved one, perhaps your neighbor...even your child. So close the curtains, grab your chai and get ready to read spine-chilling tales based on true events.